Wonder With Me

Also From Kristen Proby

Bayou Magic:
Shadows
Spells

The Big Sky Series:
Charming Hannah
Kissing Jenna
Waiting for Willa
Enchanting Sebastian

Kristen Proby's Crossover Collection:
Soaring With Fallon: A Big Sky Novel by Kristen Proby
Wicked Force: A Wicked Horse Vegas/Big Sky Novella by Sawyer
Bennett
All Stars Fall: A Seaside Pictures/Big Sky Novella by Rachel Van Dyken
Hold On: A Play On/Big Sky Novella by Samantha Young
Worth Fighting For: A Warrior Fight Club/Big Sky Novella by Laura
Kaye
Crazy Imperfect Love: A Dirty Dicks/Big Sky Novella by K.L. Grayson
Nothing Without You: A Forever Yours/Big Sky Novella by Monica
Murphy

The Fusion Series:
Listen To Me
Close To You
Blush For Me
The Beauty of Us
Savor You

The Boudreaux Series:
Easy Love
Easy Charm
Easy Melody
Easy Kisses
Easy Magic

Easy Fortune
Easy Nights

The With Me In Seattle Series:
Come Away With Me
Under the Mistletoe With Me
Fight With Me
Play With Me
Rock With Me
Safe With Me
Tied With Me
Burn With Me
Breathe With Me
Forever With Me
Stay With Me
Indulge With Me
Love With Me
Dance With Me
Dream With Me

The Love Under the Big Sky Series:
Loving Cara
Seducing Lauren
Falling For Jillian
Saving Grace

From 1001 Dark Nights:
Easy With You
Easy For Keeps
No Reservations
Tempting Brooke
Wonder With Me

The Romancing Manhattan Series:
All the Way
All It Takes
After All

Wonder With Me

A With Me In Seattle Novella

By Kristen Proby

1001 Dark Nights

EVIL EYE
CONCEPTS

Wonder With Me
A With Me In Seattle Novella
By Kristen Proby

1001 Dark Nights
Copyright 2019 Kristen Proby
ISBN: 978-1-970077-18-6

Foreword: Copyright 2014 M. J. Rose
Published by Evil Eye Concepts, Incorporated

Acknowledgments from the Author

Christmas is my favorite time of year. So when I was invited to write a holiday story set in my With Me In Seattle world, I jumped at the chance! I hope you love Reed, Noel, and little Piper as much as I do, and that the wonder of the season warms your heart this year, and every year. xo, Kristen

Sign up for the 1001 Dark Nights Newsletter
and be entered to win a Tiffany Key necklace.

There's a contest every month!

Go to www.1001DarkNights.com to subscribe.

**As a bonus, all subscribers can download
FIVE FREE exclusive books!**

One Thousand and One Dark Nights

Once upon a time, in the future…

*I was a student fascinated with stories and learning.
I studied philosophy, poetry, history, the occult, and
the art and science of love and magic. I had a vast
library at my father's home and collected thousands
of volumes of fantastic tales.*

*I learned all about ancient races and bygone
times. About myths and legends and dreams of all
people through the millennium. And the more I read
the stronger my imagination grew until I discovered
that I was able to travel into the stories… to actually
become part of them.*

*I wish I could say that I listened to my teacher
and respected my gift, as I ought to have. If I had, I
would not be telling you this tale now.
But I was foolhardy and confused, showing off
with bravery.*

*One afternoon, curious about the myth of the
Arabian Nights, I traveled back to ancient Persia to
see for myself if it was true that every day Shahryar
(Persian: شهريار, "king") married a new virgin, and then
sent yesterday's wife to be beheaded. It was written
and I had read that by the time he met Scheherazade,
the vizier's daughter, he'd killed one thousand
women.*

Something went wrong with my efforts. I arrived in the midst of the story and somehow exchanged places with Scheherazade — a phenomena that had never occurred before and that still to this day, I cannot explain.

Now I am trapped in that ancient past. I have taken on Scheherazade's life and the only way I can protect myself and stay alive is to do what she did to protect herself and stay alive.

Every night the King calls for me and listens as I spin tales. And when the evening ends and dawn breaks, I stop at a point that leaves him breathless and yearning for more. And so the King spares my life for one more day, so that he might hear the rest of my dark tale.

As soon as I finish a story... I begin a new one... like the one that you, dear reader, have before you now.

Prologue

~Reed~

"Mr. Taylor?"

"Yes, Becca." I sit back in my desk chair, pull my glasses from my face, and rub my tired eyes. A glance at the time tells me I've been staring at the computer for a few hours. The interruption is welcome.

"You have a visitor, sir."

I frown at my assistant, who's hovering in the doorway of my office. Becca's been with me for a couple of years. She's young and driven. And unlike most of the other assistants I've had, she's focused. She's never come on to me, and I swear she knows what I need before I do.

Becca's a gem.

And she's currently watching me with hesitation written all over her face.

"I never have visitors, unless they're scheduled appointments."

"I know. If you're busy, I can ask them to come back. But I don't think you'll want me to do that."

Now, I'm intrigued.

"No, it's fine. Send them in."

She nods and turns away, and I stand to stretch my legs as I wait for this unexpected guest to walk through the door.

I tug my suit jacket on just as a woman walks into my office, holding hands with...

A little girl.

They must have the wrong office.

"Reed Taylor?" the woman asks as she directs the child to sit in one of the two seats in front of my desk and hands her a stuffed bunny to cuddle.

"Yes, ma'am. And you are?"

"Melinda Hale. Mr. Taylor, I'm with the Department of Child Protective Services." She glances at the girl, whose head is bowed. "And this is Piper."

I shift my gaze between Ms. Hale and Piper, my eyes narrowed.

"Hello, Piper."

"Hello," the little girl whispers as she tugs the bunny to her chest. She's dressed in jeans and a hoodie from Old Navy, and her dark hair is pulled back into a long braid.

"I'm sure you're wondering why we're here."

"I'm hopeful you're about to tell me."

Ms. Hale smiles, but it doesn't reach her eyes. She pulls a file out of her briefcase and sets it on my desk, opens it, then passes me a letter.

"You should read this first."

The mystery of all of this is starting to grate on my nerves. I consider myself a patient man, but I'm also an efficient one.

Just get down to business, for Christ's sake.

I open the letter and frown as I read the words before me.

Reed,

I know this is a shock. Everything has happened so fast, and I know I should have reached out to you, but well, it seems I'm not strong enough to.

Piper is a sweet little girl. You'll love her, I promise.

Please take good care of her.

Warmly,

Vanessa

I fold the letter and look up to Ms. Hale. "Vanessa Downey?"

"That's right. Do you confirm that you had a relationship with Ms. Downey that ended roughly five years ago?"

I blow out a breath. Did I have a relationship with her? Vanessa would have liked that. I never committed to anything so permanent with her.

I did, however, date and have sex with her.

"I did."

"Mr. Taylor, Ms. Downey passed away a few days ago. She'd been sick." She glances down at Piper as the little girl scowls and squeezes her bunny tighter. "Well, all of the information is in this folder."

She closes the file and passes it to me.

My stomach is filled with lead. I know the next words about to come out of her mouth before she says them.

"Piper is your daughter, Mr. Taylor. Of course, we'll schedule a DNA test—"

"That's not necessary," I say, interrupting her. My eyes are on Piper as she hugs her bunny. "She looks just like me."

Piper looks up at me, her big, round, brown eyes a bit scared and sad.

"Actually, it's the law," the woman replies. "We have to make sure we've placed the child with a direct relative, of course. We'll be in touch, and will check in periodically until the results of the test come in."

"Fine. What about Vanessa's family?" I ask Ms. Hale without looking away from my daughter.

My daughter.

"Vanessa didn't have any immediate family," she explains. "If there are extended family members, we haven't found them."

My gaze whips to Ms. Hale's. What kind of a jerk am I that I didn't know that Vanessa didn't have family? "Who attended the funeral?"

"There hasn't been one yet," she says. "Of course, she had friends, but there hasn't been time—"

"I'll see to it."

She closes her lips and sits quietly, watching as I smile at Piper.

"Piper, I'm very sorry for your loss." I circle my desk and squat beside her, careful not to touch her. I don't know anything about children. I'm way out of my element here, but this isn't about me.

Christ, the poor child probably doesn't understand what's happening around her.

"Thank you," she says in a tiny voice. "Do you know where my mommy is?"

Well, hell.

"I'm sorry, sweetheart, but your mommy is in heaven."

Piper frowns and looks down at her bunny. "But where will I live?"

"With me," I reply immediately. Am I ready for this? Hell, no. But I run a multi-million dollar company. We'll figure this out. "If it's okay with you, you'll come live with me at my house. I think you'll like it there very much."

She seems to think it over, and then nods her dark little head. "Okay."

Chapter One

~Noel~

"Why do you sound like you're having sex?"

I frown at my assistant's question as I reach for the door of my favorite coffee place, my phone pressed to my ear. "Because I'm late, so I'm running, and I haven't had a chance to go to the gym lately. Stop judging me."

I sit in a chair to finish my call, rather than try to multi-task. Besides, I like the barista, and I enjoy talking with her, so I'll wait until I'm off the phone to place my order.

"No judging," Alison insists. "I don't go to the gym either. Okay, so we have a request for a consult that came in this morning."

"I don't have time," I say immediately. "Ask someone else."

"They requested you, specifically. Apparently, you came recommended."

"It'll have to happen after the first of the year," I reply, taking a deep breath. The smell of coffee is divine. And I haven't had my first of a dozen cups yet today. "I'm booked, and it's almost Christmas, Ali."

"I know, but that's the point. He wants his house decorated for Christmas. And he's willing to pay. A lot."

She rattles off a number, and I feel my eyes go wide. "Why so much?"

"Who cares?" she asks, laughing.

"Okay, listen." I mentally take stock of my afternoon. I guess I won't be getting that massage I've been longing for, after all. "I have two hours at four this afternoon. That's the only time I can do it if he wants it done now."

"Awesome," Ali says happily. "Now, don't forget…"

She reminds me of my appointments for the day, and when she finishes, I say, "Are you done, Mom? Because I'm already late, and if I don't get my coffee, I might go all murder-death-kill on someone."

"Happy holidays to you, too," Ali says, laughing before she hangs up. I mentally juggle the schedule and hurry up to the counter.

"Hey, Noel." I'm greeted with a wide smile.

"Hey, Shannon," I say, smiling in return. "I'll have—"

"Your usual," she says, passing it over. "I saw you come in, and you look like you're in a hurry."

"You're amazing, and I adore you," I gush as I accept the cup of steamy goodness and pass her my card. Cherry Street Coffee House is, ironically, *not* on Cherry Street, but rather on First Avenue West, just around the block from my condo. And it's my favorite spot for coffee, and sometimes, for something sweet.

"I know," Shannon says, winking. "Here's a scone, as well. On me."

"You don't have to do that."

"You spend more money in here than either of us wants to count," she says, shaking her head. "A scone now and then is the least I can do. Have a great day."

"Back atcha, friend. Oh!" I turn back to her. "How's Angela?"

"Settling in," Shannon says. She took in a foster child about two months ago, and it's been a tough time for both Shannon and the sixteen-year-old. "Every day is a little better."

"I'm glad. Let me know if you need anything."

I wave and hurry out into the brisk, late-autumn air. It's the first week of December, and cooler days have settled over Seattle, making the leaves crisp. They crunch under my feet as I hurry down the sidewalk to my first appointment, which happens to be, conveniently, just down the street from my condo.

I've been an interior designer in Seattle for a decade, and I feel like I finally came into my own over the past couple of years. I've gone from working for a firm to co-owning my own with two other women that I adore.

We can't keep up with the demand. We surpassed our five-year goals in just nine months.

It's been incredible, to say the least. And it's how I'm able to afford a gorgeous condo in the Belltown neighborhood of Seattle. My home is my favorite portfolio of my work. I busted my ass—and my wallet—making it a masterpiece.

If this new, generous client wants Christmas work done, that should be easy enough. I'll draw up a design for some trees, lights, garlands, and have a crew make it come to life. If I'm lucky, it'll only take a couple of days' work on my part, and our firm will be much richer.

It's definitely worth the late nights and early mornings.

It might even be worth missing out on my massage this afternoon. I usually have a weekly standing appointment, but I've had to cancel three weeks in a row. If I keep this up, my therapist will fire me.

That would be a damn shame.

I sip my coffee and breathe deeply, enjoying the crisp air. Everyone else I know loves summer so much, but I enjoy autumn in Washington the best. Especially on days like today, with the sun shining and the air cool.

With a happy, optimistic mood, and the caffeine rolling through my veins, I hurry in for my first meeting of the day.

* * * *

So, basically, I'm just running late all day, and there are few things higher on my pet peeve list than people who always run late.

I'm prompt. It's a matter of respect and courtesy.

But today? Today, the gods have it out for me.

After my first meeting, which ran long, I caught my heel in a crack in the sidewalk, it breaking in the process, and I had to hurry home to change. I allowed myself exactly twenty-seven seconds to mourn the loss of those Guccis, then hurried back out for a lunch meeting.

Which also ran long.

I'm doomed because now I'm sitting in traffic, making my way north to the super fancy Magnolia neighborhood of Seattle. It's near the water, and based on the address—and what the client is willing to pay—I'm excited to see the house.

If I can ever get there.

I blow a breath through my lips and tap my fingers on the steering wheel. Finally, once I pass a fender-bender on the right, traffic loosens up, and I'm only one minute late when I pull into the driveway.

Thank goodness.

I gather my bag and iPad and hurry to the front door. I ring the bell and wait, but no one answers.

So I try again.

Still, no answer.

Am I at the right address? Did they cancel and Ali forgot to tell me? Am I going crazy?

I pull out my phone and text Alison.

Me: *Did you confirm my 4:00 appt?*

I tap my toe and wait, longing for the massage I should be getting right now, as Ali replies.

Ali: *Yes! He's expecting you. His name is Reed.*

"Huh," I mutter, looking around. "Reed's not here."

The house is a glorious Cape Cod-style home, and it does indeed look out over Puget Sound. Ideas are already taking shape for the outside. With a landscape architect and an electrician, I could turn this into a stunning work of art.

But Reed's not answering.

So I turn back to my Lexus. Just as I do, I hear a child yelp in either delight or pain from the side of the house. I walk around, investigating, and find a little brunette girl with the sweetest face I've ever seen laughing hysterically. A man, with the same dark features, is holding her, blowing raspberries into her neck.

"You defied the king!" he yells, tickling her.

"The king is dumb!" she yells back, earning more raspberries.

I stand back, not wanting to interrupt, and smile in delight at the fun display before me. I should clear my throat or something to get their attention, but I'm enjoying them too much.

"You have to 'pologize," the girl says as she races away from him, but doesn't try very hard to outrun him. She wants to get caught. "You have to 'pologize to the princess."

"The princess was bad," he says with a laugh. "And you're too cute to punish."

He glances up and catches my gaze with his, and we both pause.

"I'm sorry to eavesdrop, your highness," I begin and curtsy. "I'm Noel, the interior designer you have a consult with this afternoon."

"Oh, shit," he says, checking the time, then points to the child. "Do *not* repeat that."

"Shit," she says gleefully and breaks out into a dance.

He sighs, rubs his hand down his face, and then shrugs a shoulder. "I'm Reed," he says, extending his hand for mine. I try to ignore the sizzle that runs up my arm at the contact.

Try being the operative word, because this guy is *hot*.

If you look tall, dark, and handsome up in the dictionary, there's likely a photo of Reed Taylor right there.

"Noel," I repeat. "And who is this lovely lady?"

"Princess Piper," she says with a sweet smile. "But you can call me Piper."

"Well, hello there, Piper."

"Her babysitter was sick today," Reed says and shrugs. "So I had to work from home."

"And your wife? Will she be joining us?" I ask.

Piper's smile falls, and Reed clears his throat.

"I'm not married," he says simply, and I immediately feel like a complete asshole.

"I'm sorry. I shouldn't have assumed." I shuffle my feet. "Shall we get started?"

"Yes, that would be great." He gestures for me to join him at a beautiful outdoor living area, with the best view of the Sound I've seen in a long time. "The fire is going, but if it's too chilly for you, we can go inside."

"No, this is great." I sit across from him and smile as Piper sits next to him and leans her head on his shoulder. "You sure are a beautiful girl."

"Thanks," she says quietly. "My mommy went to heaven, so then I had to live with Daddy."

I blink rapidly, not sure what to say to that.

"I'm sorry," Reed says, his voice perfectly calm. "She's four and—"

"No need to apologize," I assure him. "I'm so happy that you have your daddy to live with."

"Me, too," Piper says.

"Now, my assistant tells me that you're in the market for some

Christmas decorations."

"That's right," Reed says with a nod. "This is Piper's first Christmas with me, and I want to make it special. I do not, however, have an eye for decorating. Nor do I own any of the appropriate materials."

"You don't have any decorations in the attic?" I ask.

"No. I don't generally celebrate the holidays. I'm usually too busy working."

So many questions swirl around in my mind. What happened to Piper's mom? Why is this his first Christmas with Piper?

Why do I want to have my way with my client? I've worked for handsome men before. This isn't my first rodeo.

"Just from seeing the outside of your home, I have ideas," I say and smile. "I love the Cape Cod style. Do you want interior and exterior décor?"

"Yes. All of it."

"What color scheme—?"

"I don't mean to be rude," Reed interrupts, "but this is why I hired you. I don't know what the best colors are, or anything else. I run a finance company, so I can invest money for you, but I can't help you decorate my home."

"Understood," I say with a nod. "You never know how hands-on a client wants to be."

"Consider my hands *off,*" he says. "At least, where the Christmas décor is concerned."

My eyes meet his. If I'm not mistaken, Reed is flirting with me.

Perhaps the attraction is mutual.

Too bad. I have a job to do here, and I'm entirely too busy to start something with a single dad.

Too much baggage for me.

"What about you, Piper?" I ask, catching the young girl's attention. "Do you have any special requests?"

She frowns as if giving it a great deal of thought, which I find completely charming. "Can we have bunnies?"

"Bunnies?"

She nods happily. "I like bunnies."

"Christmas bunnies will certainly make their appearance this year. I'll leave you my card. My cell number is on there, and you are welcome to call or text with any questions. In the meantime, I'll get some designs drawn up and emailed to you for approval."

"Great," he says with a nod.

"And, once approved, my crew will come to make it all happen. It should only take them a couple of days, tops."

"You won't be here for that?" Reed asks and frowns.

"No, they usually have very detailed instructions to follow, and I'm just in the way."

"I'd like you here," he says as if that settles everything. "I'll pay an extra fee if need be."

"There's no need to pay extra, and there's really no need for me to be here."

"I'll triple what I'm paying you."

I sit back, confused. "Reed, this seems unnecessary."

"I'm paying for your services, and I'd like you to be here, personally, to oversee the project from start to finish."

He doesn't waver. If I decline, my firm loses a lot of money. If I accept, I lose more time and sleep, trying to cram even more into my days.

"I'll make it work," I say at last.

"Yay!" Piper says with a happy smile. "Christmas bunnies."

Chapter Two

~Reed~

Noel came highly recommended for her work. From several people, actually. And watching her as she surveys the inside of my home, I can see why. She has a sharp eye, a quick wit, and I can see that her wheels are turning at crazy-high speeds.

She's here to do a job, no more, and no less.

And yet, I'm more attracted to her than I've been to anyone in months. Maybe ever.

Since Piper came into my life just a couple of months ago, I haven't had time to notice anything. I work, I spend time with my daughter, and then, the next day, I do it all again.

But now, with Noel in my house, I'm noticing.

"Who decorated your home?" Noel asks in the kitchen. She's using a camera to take photos of the rooms, and looks at me over the lens.

"I bought it like this," I say and smile. "Furniture and all. So I'd have to ask the real estate agent. Why do you ask?"

She purses her lips and shakes her head. "It just doesn't feel like *you*. And I know that sounds odd, considering I just met you, but it's quite cold. There's no color in here."

"I spilled juice on the couch," Piper admits. "And my mom always used to say that white furniture isn't good with kids around."

"She probably had a point," Noel says with a wink. "The layout is brilliant, showing off the view." She points to the accordion windows that open to the outdoor living space, and the view of the water beyond.

"But the furniture is white, the rugs are white. *Everything* is white."

"It's clean," I offer.

"It's cold." She wanders over to the staircase. "Will I be working upstairs?"

"Everywhere," I confirm. I want Piper to have the best Christmas of her young life. After everything she's been through this year, she deserves it. My daughter takes two of my fingers in her hand as we climb the stairs behind Noel and my heart catches. It still takes my breath away when she reaches for me, climbs in my lap or kisses my cheek. Piper is an affectionate little girl, which is something I've had to get used to, but I wouldn't have her any other way.

"I want to show you *my* room," Piper announces, pushing her way to the front and leading Noel down the hall.

Her room is across from mine, so I can hear her if she needs me. I'd originally put her down the hall, but that first night here in the house she had a horrible dream, and I couldn't get to her fast enough.

I moved her things here, across from my room, the next morning.

"Oh my goodness," Noel says from the threshold. "Piper, this is beautiful."

"I got to pick it out myself," Piper says proudly.

My daughter's room looks like a princess threw up all over it. Pink upon pink upon pink flows everywhere, from her bedding, to the carpet, to the wall color. Her bed is a full-size canopy, with flowy curtains hanging down. I had a mural of happy flowers and butterflies painted on one wall.

"Finally, a room that a girl can get comfortable in," Noel says, then sends me an apologetic smile. "Sorry. I don't mean that to sound as bad as it does, it's just this room is absolutely perfect for a little girl."

"No offense taken," I say as I lean my shoulder on the doorjamb and watch as Piper shows off her books and her dolls.

Noel walks to the double doors that lead out to a deck.

"It's locked from the top, so little miss here can't get herself into trouble." I walk over and reach above Noel, feeling the heat of her back against my front, and pull the lock free, then open the double doors. We feel the air whoosh in.

"Absolutely beautiful," Noel breathes. "Piper, you hit the jackpot with this bedroom."

"What does that mean?" my daughter asks, making me grin. I adore this little girl more than I ever thought possible.

"It means you're a lucky princess," I reply and watch as her face lights up.

"Yeah, Mr. Bunny and I like it here," she says, and I can't help the wide smile that spreads over my face. I can't imagine my life without her, and I'm relieved that she's happy here with me.

"I think a Christmas tree should go right here, in front of these doors since it's about to be winter, and the doors will stay closed anyway," Noel suggests as she snaps a photo.

"Good idea," I say with a nod.

"What about your room?" Noel asks.

"What about it?"

"Will I be decorating it, as well?"

"Oh, I don't think that's necessa—"

"Yes," Piper interrupts. "Daddy, you *have* to."

"I guess I am," I say and laugh as we walk across the hall to the master.

It's a big room, with masculine furniture. I only sleep here, and I haven't had any guests since Piper came to live with me. Much to my surprise, I haven't missed having the companionship of a warm woman in my bed.

"I have a plan for this, as well," Noel says, her eyes shining as she approaches the French doors that match the ones in Piper's room. "Do you share this deck?"

"Yes, it spans the house."

"Excellent," Noel says.

"I don't mean to tell you how to do your job, but shouldn't you be writing this down?"

Noel smiles, and it hits me in the gut. "I have a strong memory. I won't forget. Plus, I have the photos."

We wander through the rest of the house, and once we're back in the living area, I act on impulse.

"Stay for dinner," I offer.

"Oh." Noel blinks, and if I'm not mistaken, her cheeks flush. "Thank you for the offer, but I need to get back to my office and get to work on this. It's an unexpected extra project, and I'd like to stay on track, maybe even get ahead."

"I understand." Of course.

She's here to do a job, not entertain you and your daughter, you idiot.

"I should have the design emailed in a day or two," she adds.

"Daddy, can I watch the iPad?" Piper asks.

"Sure." I hold a finger up to Noel. "Give me one minute to get her situated."

Noel nods and watches as I get Piper settled on the couch with my iPad and a cup of Goldfish to snack on.

"I'll walk you out," I offer, leading Noel to the doorway.

"Your home is seriously beautiful," she says as we walk outside and toward her little black car. "How long have you lived here?"

"About six weeks," I reply, making her stop and turn to me with wide, golden eyes.

"Six weeks?"

I nod and brush my hand through my hair, which reminds me that I need a haircut. But who has time?

"Piper came to live with me two months ago. I had a condo in the city, which was perfect because that's where my office is, but it's not a place for a little girl to grow up. She needs a yard and a neighborhood. So, the condo is for sale, and I found this house and moved us in. It was convenient that it came furnished."

"Wow," she says. "Well, I'm happy to work on this project for you, and if, after the holidays, you want to do some redecorating, I can help you with that, too."

Unable to stop myself, I reach out and tuck a strand of her soft, honey-colored hair behind her ear. "Thank you. I may take you up on that."

She clears her throat and turns to her car. "Okay, then. I'll be in touch."

"Drive safe."

She nods and lowers herself into her car, starts the engine, and pulls away, leaving me standing in the driveway long after she's gone.

I tip my head back and look up at the sky. The sun is getting ready to set, something Piper and I always watch together.

But for this second, I take a deep breath and wonder if I know what I'm doing.

No. No, I don't. I didn't ever plan to be a father. But here I am, doing it every day. One day at a time. *Learning* one day at a time. Because to be honest, the first couple of weeks were a disaster. I didn't know what to feed a child, or that she should only get screen time for a bit each day.

I've been reading all of the books on parenting I can get my hands on, pouring through blog posts, and calling my own mother for advice.

I walk inside, close and lock the door, and watch silently as Piper sings along with a song that's playing on the iPad. She's clutching that bunny to her side, and every once in a while, she pulls up one ear to her nose to sniff.

Roughly sixty days have gone by since I found out that I'm a father, and since she came to be with me.

She's the center of my world. The best thing I ever did. And I didn't even *know*.

Piper glances up and smiles.

"Come sing with me."

"Later. It's almost time for the sunset."

"Oh, we don't wanna miss it!" She jumps off the couch, runs to me, and grabs my hand, then leads me out to the edge of the patio. "Let me hold you."

That's code for *pick me up*. So I do, and hold her close as we watch the sun slide into the Pacific.

"Do it again," she whispers when it's gone.

"Tomorrow," I promise her.

* * * *

"Tell me if I'm pissing you off."

I'm sitting in my best friend and business partner's office. Elijah and I have been friends for a long damn time.

"Trust me, I don't have issues with telling you when you're pissing me off," he says with a laugh and leans back in his chair.

"I've been gone more than I'm here lately, and that's not—"

"Like you," he finishes for me. "I don't know if you noticed, but you've taken on a daughter you knew nothing about, moved to the 'burbs, and you're figuring it all out."

"I appreciate your willingness to be flexible, but we still have a business to run."

"And we're running it," he says and shrugs. "You're still putting in fifty-plus hours a week, Reed. You're just doing a lot of it from your home office. And that's fine."

"So you're not pissed."

"Nope." He shakes his head. "Have you found a full-time nanny yet?"

"Still looking," I mumble. "Half of these girls are just that. *Girls.* Barely old enough to have a driver's license. I'm not going to allow my daughter to ride in cars with them."

"No. I wouldn't either."

"I tried to talk my grandma into moving here. I offered her a lot of money, too."

Elijah's brows climb. "She turned you down? I don't believe it. The sun rises and sets where you're concerned."

"She hasn't been feeling well," I say with a sigh. "And I think she has a boyfriend."

He barks out a laugh. "Go, Grandma."

"Piper's in preschool half the day, and she's in daycare until four. I guess until I find a nanny, I'll have to continue leaving here by three-thirty every day to get her. I'll have Becca schedule all of my appointments for the mornings, and I'll work from home the rest of the day."

"It's the holiday season," he reminds me. "Most people are too preoccupied with shopping and parties right now to worry about investments and stocks. It's a slow time of year."

"It's year-end," I remind him.

"Yeah, and that's a bitch. But we have intelligent staff. This is why we *own* the company, so we can delegate. You need to do that more."

"I have a feeling I'll be doing it a lot over the next few weeks. But, hopefully, the dust will settle soon."

"It will. You'll fall into a routine. I have to say, I never thought I'd see the day that you'd be a daddy. I definitely didn't see it happening like this."

"Me either."

"How are you doing with all of these changes?" Elijah asks, his face somber. I know that he's the one person in the world I can be perfectly honest with, and he won't judge me.

"It's been a lot," I admit and brush my hand down my face. God, I'm tired. "I'm still overwhelmed, and maybe a little in shock."

"You find out you have a four-year-old child out there you didn't know about, and she's now your responsibility?" he says, shaking his head. "Of course you're in shock. I'd be in shock until she's eighteen."

I laugh. "I'm taking it one day at a time. She's the sweetest little thing. Vanessa clearly instilled manners in her, and she's easygoing. I'm crazy about her."

"I can see it all over your face," he says. "I'm happy for you, man. I really am."

My phone, sitting on Elijah's desk, lights up with a notification.

Incoming email from Noel.

"I have to take this. I'll see you later. Thanks for being understanding."

"You're welcome. Oh, and let me know if you ever need a sitter. I'm sure my mom would love to spend time with Piper. Maybe that'll get her off my back to have kids for a while," he says as I stand.

"Not a bad idea." I grin and walk from his office to mine.

I pull up the email from Noel on my desktop and sit back in awe as I page through the images she sent.

She has some kind of software that she uploaded the house photos into, and then she went through and added the decorations, so I can see what it'll look like when it's finished.

It's stunning. Christmas trees in every room, garland, lights. Bunnies.

Piper is going to flip.

Let me know if you have any questions is written at the bottom of the email.

Rather than reply, I pick up the phone and call her cell number.

"This is Noel," she says.

"Hi, it's Reed."

"You got my email."

"I did."

"Do you have any questions?"

"Yes. For starters, how in the hell did you do this? It's gorgeous."

Just like you.

"I'm glad you like it." I can hear the smile in her voice, and I long to be with her.

"When will you get started on it?"

"Tomorrow, actually. If that works for your schedule."

"I can make that work. What time should I expect you?"

"The crew will be there at eight. I'll meet them there."

"Great. I'll see you then."

We hang up, and I scroll through the photos again. If the finished product is half as beautiful as what she's given me here, Piper will be over the moon.

I can't wait.

Chapter Three

~Noel~

I have my coffee, extra-large, and I'm ready to tackle this day. If all goes as planned, in just three days, Reed's house will look like Santa himself lives there.

Traffic headed out of the city isn't too bad this morning since I'm driving opposite of rush-hour traffic, so getting up to his place should only take me about fifteen minutes.

"Long enough to enjoy this coffee," I mutter to myself just as my phone rings. My sister's name comes up on my car's screen. I click accept on my steering wheel. "Hello there."

"Hey, I was hoping I'd catch you before you started in with your meetings today," Joy says. I can hear dogs barking around her, but that's not unusual, given that my sister is a successful veterinarian in Seattle.

"You did catch me. I'm on my way to a job. What's up?"

"I think we should do family dinner on Sunday with Dad. It's been a few weeks since we've seen you."

"I know." I sigh and take a sip of my coffee. "It seems that everyone in the Seattle metro area suddenly wants their house decorated."

"This is the time of year everyone has parties, so of course they want their homes to look nice."

"You have a good point," I concede and wonder why I didn't think of that. "But I'll make time for dinner on Sunday. How is Daddy? Have you talked to him?"

"He's good. He brought Nancy in for a check-up yesterday, and he looks happy. He said he has a date on Saturday."

I sit stunned, staring at the red taillights ahead of me.

"Noel?"

"Yeah."

"Did you hear me?"

"I think so. Dad has a *date?*"

"I was pretty surprised, too," she says. "But he seems excited about it."

"Mom's only been gone for three years."

"That's a long time, Noel," she says softly. "I know it feels like yesterday, but three years is a long time."

"Well, as long as he's happy, I guess." I swallow hard, still wrapping my head around this. "We'll ask all of the questions on Sunday."

"That's my plan," Joy replies. "Okay, don't work too hard. Love you."

"Love you, too."

She ends the call, and I bite my lip. I don't know how I feel about my dad dating someone new. I guess I'll set it aside until we talk to him on Sunday.

I pull into Reed's driveway, pleased when I see that the crew, along with their big trucks and supplies, made it here before me.

With coffee in hand, I march down the driveway to the house and see Reed talking with one of the men.

"There she is," Reed says, looking relieved when he sees me.

"Great." Bob, a man I've worked with many times before, turns and smiles at me. He's old enough to be my father, but I still flirt with him relentlessly.

"Hey there, handsome," I say to Bob and pat his shoulder. "Are you all ready to go?"

"Your notes were clear, as always. My boys will get started out here right away."

"Thank you." I smile up at him, chuckle when he blushes a bit, and watch as he walks back to his truck.

"I think I'm jealous of Bob," Reed says beside me.

"Why is that?"

"He just got way more attention out of you than I've managed to do," he says. I turn to him and sip my drink.

"Well, Bob does a hell of a job, and I think he's rather adorable."

"So you like older men, then."

I shrug a shoulder, trying not to notice how broad Reed's chest looks in his blue button-down shirt, or how his forearms flex as he pushes his hands into his pockets.

Good Lord, Reed is something to write home about.

"I'm going to need you to leave," I inform him and watch as he raises an eyebrow.

"In what capacity?"

"I need you and Piper to move out of here for the few days that this will take. First, because you'll just be in the way. And second, because I want it to be a surprise when it's finished."

"You're kicking me out of my own house."

I wink up at him. "Yes. I am."

I turn to talk to my interior crew, but my toe catches on a rock, and I pitch forward, my coffee flying out of my hands and splattering all over Reed's driveway.

Strong arms catch me, keeping me from falling on my face, and all I can do is stare longingly at the coffee steaming off the concrete.

"Damn it."

"Are you okay?"

"I'm fine. Thanks for catching me."

He has strong hands. Firm arms. A tight grip around my waist.

I wonder how he'd hold me if we were naked, and—

I shake my head, stopping those thoughts before they have a chance to go *anywhere* else.

"Come on," he says, taking my hand and pulling me behind him.

"Where are we going?"

"I'm taking you for a new coffee."

"I can't, I have to talk to Jean about the stairway, and—"

"They're just unloading and organizing. It will take a while. They don't need you yet."

"How do you know what they need?"

He stops and turns to me with a huff. "Are you always this obstinate when a man tries to buy you coffee?"

"When said man tries to pry me away from my job site? Yes. You hired me to make your home beautiful, not to go to a café with you."

"You're stubborn."

And with that, he bends over and slings me over his shoulder, carrying me easily—and in front of my crew—to his car.

"Attaboy!" Bob yells, giving Reed a thumbs-up.

"You're not helping!" I call back to him, but he just smiles at me.

Finally, Reed sets me next to his boxy Mercedes SUV and opens the passenger door. "Get in."

"You just made me a laughing stock in front of my crew."

Reed frowns and looks around the driveway. "The only one looking this way is Bob, and he's not laughing. He looks proud of me."

I sigh in agitation and get into the car before I do what I really want to do: stomp on his foot and march away.

I will *not* admit that being carried by him, having his arms wrapped around me twice in the span of two minutes, made my core tighten.

I won't give him the satisfaction.

"There's a Starbucks up the road."

I wrinkle my nose.

"Not a Starbucks girl?"

"It'll do in a pinch. Cherry Street coffee is my favorite, but they're at least thirty minutes away."

"I'll remember that," he murmurs and drives away from his house. "It's my fault you spilled the coffee. The least I can do is replace it."

"It's not your fault I tripped on a rock."

"It was *my* rock."

I shake my head and glance over at him. "I think we're both stubborn."

"Me? No way." He laughs and takes my hand in his, linking our fingers. Before I can pull away, he kisses the back of my hand.

"Reed, you're a client."

"Yes, I am."

"It's unprofessional for me to have any other sort of relationship with you."

"If you don't like what I'm doing, all you have to do is say so, and I will never bother you again," he says clearly, all humor gone from his face. "I have no interest in harassing you or making you feel uncomfortable."

"I'm not uncomfortable."

"Good. I'm not a jerk, Noel. Now, why do you need us to leave the house again?"

"You heard me the first time."

"Tell me again, I like your voice."

I can't help the laugh that comes out at that statement. He grins at me. "There, I like that very much."

"I need you both to relocate for a couple of days so you're out of our way, and so I can do a grand reveal when it's all finished. I think it'll be fun for Piper."

"I do, too. Well, the condo hasn't sold yet, so we'll go there for a couple of days."

"Thanks. We should have it all wrapped up in less than three working days. There's a lot to do, but the crew is organized and quick. I think you're going to love it."

"If it's as good as the photos you sent, we'll never want to take it down."

I smile, pleased that he liked my proposal. I worked my ass off on it, and the design came easily to me, as if I'd done it many times before.

Reed pulls the car into the Starbucks parking lot, and we go inside. My coffee order is very different here than at Cherry Street.

"Grande light roast with plenty of room for cream, please."

Reed stares down at me. "That's it?"

"That's it."

"Okay. I'll have the same, but make mine a medium roast."

He pays for our coffees, and once we've added the right amount of cream and sweetener, we're back on the road to his house.

"I could have sworn I smelled caramel in the coffee you spilled," he says.

"You did. My order at Cherry Street is different. They use a really great, homemade caramel."

"I'll have to try it sometime," he says and smiles. "My condo isn't far from there."

My gaze quickly swings to his. "Really? *My* condo is just around the corner from the First Avenue West location."

"I'm about a block over." He grins at me. "How convenient."

I decide to let that comment slide. I'm *so* attracted to him, but I don't have time to get involved right now. The whole client thing isn't such a big deal because this job is only a couple of days, but the time factor *is* a thing. "Thank you for this. I appreciate it."

"You're welcome." He sets his drink in the cup holder and reaches for my hand again. "Now, before we get back, I want to be up-front and say, right here and now, that I'm incredibly attracted to you, Noel. I'd like to date you."

I cough on the sip of light roast I just took and then stare at him. "Well, I give you props for your honesty. And in that spirit, I'll tell you right here and now that I don't have time to date you—or anyone else for that matter."

"I'm not concerned about anyone else," he says, his voice perfectly calm as he watches the road in front of us. "I'm only concerned with me, and you're just going to have to make time because *not* seeing you isn't an option for me."

I'm still staring at him, and then I bust up laughing.

"I don't know what you find funny."

"This whole thing," I say, wiping the tears from my eyes. "*Make* time? How do you propose I do that? There are only twenty-four hours in a day, and I work roughly sixteen of those hours. So when you find a way to add some minutes to the day, you let me know."

He pulls into the driveway, but before I can open the door, he says, "Wait for me."

I've never been the kind of girl attracted to the alpha type. That's not to say I want a pushover, but the whole, *I'm man, I tell you what to do* thing has never appealed to me.

Yet here I am. Waiting.

He opens my door, offers his hand, and when I'm standing, he closes the door and leans into me, effectively pinning me against his expensive automobile.

I absolutely *do not* want to push him away. Is he being bossy? Yes. Is he sexy as hell? Also, yes.

He plants one hand on the car and dips his head next to mine.

"We make time for the things that matter," he whispers into my ear. "Like, just now, we carved out fifteen minutes to go and get a coffee. I had you all to myself. We had a conversation, a harmless flirtation. I even made you laugh. If all I can get is fifteen minutes here and there, so be it."

He kisses my neck—*my freaking neck*—and then winks at me as he walks away.

"I'll be out of your hair in about ten minutes," he tosses over his shoulder as I struggle to breathe.

Oh my God, I'm turned on. If there weren't people around, I'd be fanning my face.

Damn him!

I. Don't. Have. Time.

* * * *

It's been a crazy day.

Reed's house is looking fantastic. If I get lucky, it may be finished by tomorrow evening.

Maybe.

But if not, it'll still be done on time, and that's all I can really ask for.

I've just walked into my condo, kicked my heels off, and opened the fridge for the bottle of white I have on hand.

Sometimes a girl just needs a glass of wine.

Or two.

I smirk and pull the cork out of the bottle and fill a glass half full. On my way into my bedroom, where I'm headed to change, I get a text.

From Reed.

My body is still tingling from that little encounter in his driveway this morning.

He's potent.

And hot as hell.

And I'm reminded as I stare down at the silly photo of Reed and Piper sticking their tongues out at the camera, that he's a dad.

I don't overthink it as I flip on the camera and snap a quick picture of me sticking out my tongue at them and send it off.

Rather than just changing my clothes, I think I want a hot shower. I worked hard today, hanging garlands and decorating Christmas trees, and my muscles are weary.

I usually take my phone into the bathroom with me so I can listen to podcasts while I bathe, and this time is no different. I've just started my favorite show, *My Favorite Murder*, which never fails to both creep me out and make me laugh when another text comes through.

Reed: *We're at my condo in the city, having pizza for dinner. You should join us.*

I smile at the mental image of the two of them eating pizza with the skyline in the background. I have no idea what Reed's condo looks like, or even where it is for sure, but I like the image in my mind.

Me: *Thanks for the invitation. I'm in the shower, so I think I'm in for the night. I hope you enjoy your dinner!*

Several minutes pass. The hosts of my podcast talk about a serial killer in Hawaii as I lather up my hair and then rinse it. Finally, when I've finished with the shower and I'm drying off, another text comes through from Reed.

Reed: *It's not fair to tell me you're in the shower when I'm hanging out with my four-year-old daughter.*

I laugh and snap a photo of myself in my towel and send it off to him. Yes, I'm flirting with a client. No, I don't have time for him.

Yes, this could get messy. I'm well aware of the what-ifs and how it could all go wrong.

But you know what? I don't care. I'm not usually a risk-taker. I always follow the rules.

But something tells me Reed's worth it. And you only live once, right?

Chapter Four

~Reed~

"One more book."

Piper looks up at me with pleading, brown eyes, but I remain strong in my resolve.

"I read *one more book* twice," I remind her and scoot off of her bed, then tuck her in. "And you can hardly keep your eyes open."

"I'm not sleepy."

Her eyes are closed now, her face softening as slumber begins to take over. I take a moment to watch her, the way her dark lashes lie on the soft white skin of her cheeks, her pink lips slightly parted. Her bunny is tucked under her chin.

My daughter is the prettiest little thing I've ever seen.

I turn off the light and quietly walk to the door, leaving it ajar several inches so I can hear her if she needs me.

The lights of Seattle wink at me through the glass of the windows. I was so excited when I bought this condo five years ago. I never thought I'd leave it. Imagined the heart of the hustle and bustle of the city was exactly where I'd always be.

I didn't do relationships and, in hindsight, I regret the way I treated Vanessa. I never lied to her, she knew the score, and if you'd asked me at the time, I would have said I wasn't doing anything wrong. She eventually got tired of me and moved on. At least, that's what I thought.

But I didn't do anything to stop her.

I also didn't respect her enough to ask her if she was okay. I was too self-absorbed to think of it.

Having Piper with me has jerked me out of that self-centered mindset. Made me consider more than my job, my needs. It's made me have more care with those around me.

Jesus, I feel like I was sleep-walking for the first thirty years of my life, and I'm only now fully awake.

I'm not proud of it. If I think of a man treating Piper the way I did Vanessa, well…it makes me want to punch a hole in the wall.

I wish Vanessa were still here so I could apologize to her. She deserved better than what I gave her.

I hear Piper cough, so I go poke my head in to check on her. But she doesn't wake up, she just turns to her side and goes right back to sleep.

The only thing I can do for Vanessa now is to make sure Piper is not only well taken care of, but also loved more than anything. And it's more than a little surprising for me to admit that I've fallen more in love with Piper than I ever thought I could.

She's mine. My flesh and blood.

There are days that it feels like it's still sinking in.

My phone buzzes with a text from Noel, and I sit on the couch, facing the lights of the city, and smile at my screen.

Noel: *How was your pizza?*

Rather than text her back, I call her.

"If the story about pizza warrants a phone call, it must not have been good," she says into my ear. She sounds sleepy.

"Are you in bed?" I ask her softly.

"I'm lying here reading. It's a little early for sleep, even for me."

"What are you reading?" I ask her.

"It's a romance novel."

"I probably haven't read it." I feel my lips twitch.

"No, I don't think you have. So how was the pizza?"

"It was fine. The conversation I was having with a certain interior designer was better than the pizza."

"Yeah? How come?"

"I got naked photos of her."

She laughs. "I know for certain I didn't send you a naked photo."

"You were in a towel, that's close enough. I can use my imagination."

She sighs in my ear and even that quiet sound has something stirring inside me. "You're quite the flirt, you know that, right?"

"I never really have been before," I admit. "But I like talking with you. What are you doing tomorrow?"

"Hmm, let me check my schedule. Ah, yes, that's right, I'm *decorating your house.*"

"Do you have a tree picked out for the living room yet?"

"Yes, I have all of the trees."

"Is it real?"

She's quiet for a moment. "No, they're all fake trees. They can be reused that way, and you don't have to worry about watering them. Also, no fire hazard."

"Well, I think Piper should have a real tree in the living room."

"I don't have—"

"And you should go with us tomorrow to pick one out."

I hear her sigh again. I lean my head back on the couch, wishing she were sitting next to me rather than a block away.

"Reed, I have a full day ahead of me."

"Duck out around four," I urge her. "That's not too early. I'll pick up Piper, and we can go get a tree. We're learning to *make* time, remember?"

"Right," she says. "Okay. I'll leave at four, just for you guys."

"Thank you, Noel."

"You're welcome."

* * * *

"There's *snow!*" Piper exclaims as I help her out of the truck I borrowed from Elijah and set her on the ground. She's bundled up in boots and a pink snowsuit, and her face is lit up like the Fourth of July. "I've never played in the snow."

"You've never seen snow?" Noel asks, and Piper shakes her head no.

"Piper and her mother lived on the coast, so they never got any snow over there," I say.

"I love snow," Noel says. I picked her up from my house thirty minutes ago. She wouldn't let us near the place. Instead, she met us at the end of the driveway by the road.

She's been *very* secretive when it comes to her work.

This tree farm is up near Snoqualmie, higher in elevation, where they get much more snow than the city does.

"Maybe we should leave Mr. Bunny in the truck," Noel suggests and squats next to Piper to talk to her. "You don't want him to get dirty while we play and look for a tree, do you?"

"I don't wanna leave him," Piper says as she holds him tightly against her chest. "He'll be sad."

"He can sit on the dash and watch us," Noel says. "Here, let me show you. And if you don't like it, we'll take him."

Piper begrudgingly lets Noel take the bunny. Noel sits him in the window of the truck so he's facing the tree farm.

"See? He can see everything, so he's not sad. And he's safe in there."

"He's probably warmer in there, too," I add, and Piper nods her head.

"He doesn't have a snowsuit," she says. "Okay, he can stay there, as long as he can see us. He's *never* been away from me. Ever."

Piper told me not long after she came to live with me that Vanessa gave Piper the bunny when Piper was a baby. Piper said the stuffed animal still smells like her mother.

The thought of it pulls at my heart.

We walk through the snow to talk to someone about borrowing a saw and a wagon, I buy the girls some hot chocolate, and then we're off, looking for the perfect Christmas tree.

"What about this one?" Noel asks about twenty yards down the path.

"It's not tall enough," I say, and she turns to me.

"You have a twelve-foot ceiling in that room."

"Exactly."

She laughs. "This tree has to be about eleven feet tall."

I shake my head and lead them farther down the path. Piper looks as if she's having a hard time trudging through the snow, so I lift her into the wagon and pull her behind me.

"This is fun!" Piper exclaims, drinking her little hot chocolate as

Noel and I look for a tree.

"She gets to ride," Noel mumbles.

I've got something you can ride.

Of course, I don't say that out loud, but if I have my way, I'll whisper it to her later when my daughter isn't listening to every word we say.

Finally, after about thirty minutes of looking, I find the tree I want.

"This is a *Christmas Vacation* movie tree," Noel says with a laugh.

"You're nuts. It's perfect."

"It's way too big," she insists, but then holds her hands up and steps back. "But it's your house, your tree. I just won't be held responsible when it takes up the whole room, and a squirrel comes flying out of it."

"It has a squirrel?" Piper asks, excitement in her brown eyes.

"No, honey," I say with a laugh. "No critters in this tree. Now, you ladies stand back while I cut it down."

I have to wade my way into limbs, but once I get my footing, it doesn't take long to cut the trunk and have it fall on its side.

Rather than make Piper get out of the wagon, I grip the trunk in my arms and begin to drag it.

"Isn't this what we have the wagon for?" Noel asks and grins.

"Let her ride," I say, shrugging. "You pull her, I'll drag the tree."

"You're a softie," she says, but the words are gentle, and her golden eyes shine as she reaches for the handle of the wagon. "I kind of like it."

She walks toward me, and I stop her, run my hand over her coat-covered hip, and kiss her cold forehead.

"I'm glad," I say and then step back to follow the ladies to the truck.

Noel doesn't say anything more, but she swallows hard before leading me down the path.

Once I've paid for the tree and have loaded it into the bed of the truck, we head back toward the city.

"We'll drop the tree off at the house."

"You can put it in the *garage*," Noel says sternly. "It'll warm up in there. No going inside. And don't look too hard at the outside, either."

"Yes, ma'am."

"I mean it."

"I won't look. I swear." I laugh and enjoy the ride, with Piper in the back talking to her bunny, telling him about our adventure, and Noel next to me.

She fits in so well with us, it's as if she's always been here.

I pull into the driveway, and when I open the door, she opens hers as well.

"Wait for me," I instruct her, then walk around to the passenger side of the truck. I offer her my hand and help her down to the concrete. Before she can walk away, I pin her against the door, the way I did yesterday, in this same spot. "Come to my place tonight. Have dinner with Piper and me."

"Reed, I want to—"

"Great."

"But I have—"

"Work," I finish for her. "You have to eat, and my place isn't out of the way."

I see her softening. I lean in closer and press my lips to her ear.

"I want to spend time with you. Say yes."

"Yes. I'll come."

Hopefully, I'll have her coming sooner rather than later.

I kiss her, just below her ear, and breathe in her citrus scent. Her hair is soft against my nose.

I want to crush her to me and devour her. God, I've never wanted anyone the way I want Noel.

But that's for later.

"I'll text you my address," I say as I pull back.

"I'll be there in an hour."

* * * *

"How did you know that Broadway Bar & Grill is my favorite?" Noel tosses the empty to-go containers in the trash.

"I didn't. It's *my* favorite," I reply with a smile.

"I *always* get the BLT," she continues. "And you somehow knew to get that for me. Are you stalking me?"

"I don't have time to stalk you," I reply as I lean against the countertop, watching as she tidies the kitchen. I told her she didn't have to do that, but she just shrugged and did it anyway.

Honestly, I'm too tired to argue. If the woman wants to clean the kitchen, I say, let her.

This time.

"I'm ready," Piper announces as she walks into the kitchen. She's in her jammies, ready for her nightly reading time.

"I should go," Noel says, and my stomach tightens.

I don't want her to go.

Not yet.

"I want Noel to read to me," Piper says. "Please?"

"Oh, I suppose I can do that," Noel says with a surprised smile. "Sure. Do you have a favorite book?"

"Yeah, come on," Piper says, taking Noel's hand and leading her to her temporary bedroom. I can hear their voices as they get settled on the bed.

I tidy up, putting Piper's snow suit and boots in the closet, her socks in the laundry. I reach for a damp sponge and wipe down the countertops.

Once all of that is done, I walk to the bedroom and listen as Noel finishes the first story.

"You read good," Piper says around a yawn.

"Thanks. Does your daddy read to you at bedtime?"

"Yeah, he reads good, too. I like stories. Mommy used to read to me."

"I like to read books, as well," Noel says.

"What kind of books do you like?"

"Hmm. Fairy tales for grown-ups, I guess."

"I like princess stories," Piper says and yawns again.

"I think you're ready for sleep."

"I'm not tired."

It's the same every night, and it seems it doesn't matter who's tucking her in.

Good to know.

"Goodnight, sweet girl."

I walk into the kitchen and pour two glasses of wine, just as Noel returns from Piper's room.

"She's beautiful," Noel says.

"Thank you." I pass her a glass and take a sip from mine.

"I'd like to know more about both of you."

"Well, then, let's sit and talk for a while, shall we?"

Chapter Five

~Noel~

The building Reed's condo is in isn't just down the block from mine, it's literally next door. So, walking over for dinner wasn't a hardship.

And staying to read to his daughter made me the most relaxed I've been in a long time.

These two are quickly worming their way into my heart, and it's both exhilarating and a little scary.

"What would you like to know?" Reed asks as we settle on his plush couch. I toe off my shoes and rest my feet on the ottoman in front of me, my wine cradled in my hands. Reed shifts to face me and rests his elbow on the back cushions. "I'm an open book."

"I am, too," I say before taking a sip of my wine. "I feel like I know you, but I really don't know you at all. Are you from Seattle?"

"Yes," he replies. "I grew up in Issaquah. My dad was a firefighter, and Mom was a high school principal."

"Siblings?" I ask.

"No," he says. "I'm an only child, but my best friend, Elijah, has been like a brother to me since we were in grade school. He's my business partner."

"Wow." I blink and shift so I'm facing him, one leg under the other. "You both decided to go into finance?"

"Not at first. He was going to be a pro-football player, but he got hurt in college, and his path shifted a bit. I'll admit, I'm glad."

"I bet." I smile and lay my head on my hand, my elbow also resting on the back of the couch. "I have a sister. Joy is exactly one year older than me. We were both born on Christmas Eve."

"Joy and Noel," he says and smiles.

"Christmas names. Our mom passed away a few years ago, which was hard. Dad, especially, has struggled, but I talked to my sister yesterday, and she said Dad has a date on Saturday. Maybe he's starting to heal."

"I hope he is," Reed says. His dark eyes are kind. He's watching me, truly listening.

"Me, too. Are you close to your parents?"

"I wouldn't say we're close, but we're not estranged. I see them on holidays. They don't live in Washington anymore. They haven't even met Piper yet, but I think they're planning to make a trip up after the new year."

I nod and sip my wine. "I have some personal questions, too."

"Sweetheart, if I have my way, you and I are headed for as personal as it gets, so ask all of the questions you want."

I tip up an eyebrow. "I do like your honesty."

"There's no need to be anything but honest."

"You're right. Okay, how did Piper come to be? And don't give me the whole *when a mommy loves a daddy* line."

He laughs and shakes his head. "I dated a woman for a while. I never let it get as serious as she wanted, which I know makes me sound like an ass. She broke things off, and I didn't look back. I figured she was just finished, and we both moved on with our lives. Flash forward almost five years to about two months ago. I was in my office, and a woman showed up with Piper and said, 'She's your daughter.'"

I feel my jaw drop. "No written notice? Nothing?"

"If they sent anything in writing, I never got it," he says. "The woman had a note from Piper's mom addressed to me, asking me to take care of our daughter."

"So you didn't know until two months ago that you *had* a daughter?"

"No."

"You took her in, bought her a new house, and basically turned your life upside down for her."

He frowns and looks down into his mostly empty glass. "I would have done the same if Vanessa had told me when she was pregnant. Though I probably still wouldn't have married her. Again, I know I'm an ass."

"You didn't love her," I reply, my voice calm. "That's not a crime."

"No, I suppose not."

"What happened to Vanessa?" I ask. "And why didn't she tell you? Aren't you mad at her?"

"I'm angry at her for not telling me about Piper before, yes. I missed so many years, so many *firsts* that I'll never get back. But part of me knows why she didn't tell me. Was it wrong of her? Yes, absolutely, but I think she was afraid of how I'd take the news. I can only guess that those are her reasons because she didn't leave me any other explanation. She passed from cancer," he says and sips his wine. "According to the paperwork I got, she had an aggressive form."

"I'm sorry to hear that," I reply. "Poor Piper."

"She was devastated. She still talks about her a lot, and I encourage her to. For the first couple of weeks, she was pretty depressed. Didn't want to eat much or play. She was grieving."

"Of course she was. I was twenty-six when I lost my mom, and I'm still grieving. I can't imagine being four, confused, and in a new home with a stranger."

"Exactly," he says and reaches over to take my hand in his. His skin is warm and smooth. "But she's coming out of her shell. She likes her preschool, and I have her in counseling once a week, just to make sure she's adjusting well."

"I have to tell you, I know you're new to this whole parenthood thing, but I think you're rocking it."

"You do?"

His eyes are full of hope and vulnerability, and I want to pull him in for a hug.

So I do.

I push up to my knees and gather Reed close, hugging him tightly. "I do," I whisper. "She's lucky to have you. And I can see that she loves you very much, even after just a couple of months."

His arms tighten around me, and the next thing I know, he shifts me into his lap, and the roles are reversed. Now, *he's* cradling *me*.

In those strong, muscly arms of his.

I've never wanted anyone to kiss me so badly in my life.

He slowly lowers his lips to mine and pauses, just as our mouths touch. His eyes are open, watching me as if he's waiting for me to tell him to stop.

There's no way I want to stop him.

I plunge my fingers into the thick, dark hair at the nape of his neck, and he must take that as an invitation because he goes from hot to boiling in one-point-one seconds.

His mouth is firm, and he knows his way around a girl's lips.

He cups my cheek in his palm and deepens the kiss.

A soft moan fills the air, and it takes me a minute to realize it's coming from *me*.

"You're so damn sweet," he whispers as he shifts the angle. His hand roams from my cheek, down my neck, and over my breast where my nipple strains against my bra. He gently brushes his fingers over the tight nub, and then that magical hand of his keeps roaming farther south.

He slips his finger under the waistband of the leggings I changed into before coming over here, and just when I think he's going to make it to the part of me most yearning for him, we hear a tiny voice.

"Daddy?"

I've never moved so fast in my life. We spring apart, and Reed flies to his feet.

"What's wrong, baby?"

"Are you cuddling with Noel?"

I cover my mouth and stifle a laugh.

"Yeah, we were just cuddling. Are you okay?"

"I need a drink of water."

"Okay, come with me."

Reed takes Piper to get a drink and then leads her back to bed. I put on my shoes and gather my jacket and handbag. When he returns, I see the disappointment in his eyes as he sees I'm ready to go.

"I'm sorry," he says as his shoulders slump.

"No, you have nothing to be sorry about. I had a great evening." I don't hesitate to walk to him and loop my arms around his middle, pressing my ear to his chest. "Besides, I'll see you tomorrow."

"Damn right you will. We have unfinished business."

I laugh and look up at him. "I'm finishing your *house* tomorrow. You and Piper should come around six for the grand reveal."

"We'll be there," he says. "I wish I could walk you home. I don't like the idea of you walking alone at this time of night."

"I'll be fine," I assure him. "I'm in the building next door."

"That close?"

"Yep."

"And all this time, I never met you," he murmurs as he lightly rubs the pad of his thumb across my lips.

"There are a lot of people in Seattle." I kiss his thumb and smile when his eyes darken with lust. "I'll see you tomorrow."

"Text me when you get home."

"Yes, sir."

He smirks and watches me as I walk down the hall to the elevator. His tall, lean form is the last thing I see as the doors close.

I let out a long breath and, now that I'm alone, fan my face. Damn, that man is potent. Sexy as hell, and *so* sweet with his daughter.

I'm already in deep.

* * * *

I want every detail to be perfect. The crews left about an hour ago, but I've been working my way through the house, making small adjustments and fussing here and there. I've never been so nervous for a client to see a finished product before.

At exactly six, the doorbell rings, and I take a moment to smooth my hands down my red skirt and check my hair in a mirror before I hurry to open the door.

"Welcome home," I say with a bright smile. "Before you come inside, I'd like to step out and hear your thoughts on the outside."

The sun has set, but it's not quite dark yet. The lights are on, twinkling in every tree, shrub, and on all the rocks. Red bows and garland are draped on the porch. If it would just snow for me, it would look like something out of a Currier and Ives painting.

"It's so pretty!" Piper says with excitement. "I like the lights."

"I do, too," Reed says, watching me. "Very pretty."

"You haven't even looked at the lights," I murmur, but he just flashes that slow, sexy smile that makes my stomach tighten.

"Very pretty, indeed."

"I wanna see inside," Piper says.

"Okay, let's do it." I open the door for them and immediately lead them up the stairs. "Let's begin our tour upstairs, shall we?"

More garland and ribbons weave and loop on the banister leading up the stairs. Bits and baubles in festive colors sit on the hall tables, and I took the liberty of buying winter-themed art for the walls.

"You went above and beyond," Reed says behind me.

"We've barely scratched the surface. Let's start with your dad's room," I say to Piper, wanting to keep the anticipation of her room building.

I open the door to Reed's bedroom, and he lets out a long, low whistle.

The tree standing in front of the French doors is lit and twinkling in the low light. I used burgundy and greens in his room, keeping in theme with the masculine feel of the space.

"This is great. Not too busy, not overdone," Reed says, looking around.

"No, simple and classy fits you best," I reply and feel my cheeks heat when he slides his hand into mine, linking our fingers.

"I love it."

"I'm glad."

"Now, my room!" Piper yells and hurries across the hall. She flings open the door, and then stops short, her brown eyes wide with excitement. "Wow!"

"Wow is right," Reed says when we join her.

There's a matching Christmas tree in front of her doors, but this one is draped in pink and cream-colored ribbons and ornaments, with bunnies sitting on the branches.

"So many bunnies," Piper breathes.

"Well, your wish is my command when it comes to holiday décor," I remind them both and can't help but smile as we watch Piper inspect every single bunny, holding her own precious rabbit close to her chest.

"What are these bunnies?" Piper asks, pointing next to her bed.

"Those are bunny slippers," I inform her. "You have a matching robe in the bathroom."

Piper runs into the bathroom and squeals in delight.

"You decorated the bathroom, too?" Reed asks as he looks inside.

More pink bunnies, more ribbons, and even a small tree on the corner of the vanity greet us.

"Of course." I wink down at Piper, who wraps her arms around my leg and gives me a huge hug.

"Thank you," she says.

"You're most welcome."

I show them to the guest rooms, where the design is simple and neutral, with reds, and gold and silver accents.

Then we make our way downstairs.

Each of the white kitchen cabinets have wreaths hanging on red ribbons. I brought in red blankets for the couches, pillows that say *Joy to the World* and *Naughty or Nice?*

"This should be featured in a magazine," Reed says as they take everything in.

"Look outside," Piper says, pointing to the lights strung across the outdoor living space.

Reed pushes back the accordion door, only a quarter of the way because it's quite cold today in Seattle, and we step out. We can see boats gliding over the water of the Sound, but it's the lights and the outdoor pillows on the furniture that have Piper's attention.

"I hope you like it."

Reed turns to me and pulls me in for a tight hug. Clients have hugged me in excitement before, but it's usually the female ones that do so.

Not hot, sexy men that I'm pretty sure want in my pants.

His spicy scent surrounds me. I could get lost in him.

"Why is the tree in here naked?" Piper asks as she walks back into the house.

"Good question," Reed says, looking down at me. "The living room tree doesn't have any ornaments."

"Well, this is the tree we picked out together," I say as Reed closes the glass doors. "Once Bob cut it down a bit, we got it set up."

I glance at Reed, who just narrows his eyes on me, but they're full of humor.

It was totally too big for this space.

"A girl should decorate her own Christmas tree," I say at last. "I have a box of ornaments ready to go. I'm even cooking you guys dinner, and I might have baked cookies for dessert."

Okay, so I've never baked cookies for a client before, but I couldn't help myself. I wanted everything to be just perfect, just *so*. I like spending time with them both so much, and I wanted to spend more time with them this evening, past the simple reveal of the decorations.

Piper jumps up and down in excitement, and Reed just watches me, his hands shoved into his pockets, and I wonder if I've overstepped.

I mean, he didn't invite me to stay.

"If you'd rather do this, just the two of you, I totally understand, and I'll just leave—"

Before I can finish my thought, Reed shocks me by pulling me in for a kiss. Long and slow and thorough, and when I come up for air, I glance down at Piper, who's watching us with interest.

"Your daughter—"

"Will get used to seeing me kiss you," he finishes for me. "Now, let's get started on this tree. And dinner. I'm starved. Are you hungry, honey?"

"Yes. But I wanna decorate first."

"We can do both," I say, recovering my wits. "I made appetizers, so it's easy to eat and work at the same time."

"Perfect." Reed follows me to the kitchen. "Thank you. For all of this. You killed it."

"I know." I grin and pass him a bottle of wine. "And you're welcome. Will you please open that?"

"I'm happy to. By the way, I have a holiday party for my firm on Friday. I'd like you to be my date."

I stop and stare at him. "That's in two days."

"Yep."

I nod, mentally combing through my closet. I think I have several things that will work for a holiday party. "Okay. I'm in."

"Excellent."

Chapter Six

~Noel~

"Noel, I'd like you to meet Nate McKenna, and his wife—"

"Jules!" I wrap my arms around my friend and grin at her ridiculously hot husband. I no longer feel guilty for thinking that Nate McKenna is hot. It's just common knowledge among the family that the Montgomerys, and their spouses, are stupidly attractive.

"You know each other?" Reed asks.

"Yes," Jules says and nods. "It's all by marriage, and confusing, but we know Noel well. How are you?"

"I'm great, thank you. How are you guys? How's Stella?"

"Our daughter is growing up too fast," Nate says. His hand rests protectively on Jules' waist. At well over six and a half feet tall, with broad shoulders and muscles for days, no one ever messes with Nate.

"She's getting big," Jules says and then turns her attention to Reed. "And I hear congratulations are in order for you. How is your little one?"

"Piper's great. She's with an overnight sitter for the first time since she came to live with me, and so far, I haven't received any SOS calls, so I consider that a win."

We all chuckle, and then Reed and Nate step aside to talk about business, and Jules leans in. I know this is going to be fun girl-talk.

"Tell me what's happening," she says.

I've quickly learned that Jules doesn't pull punches. She's also incredibly fun, sweet, and someone you want for a friend.

"It's brand new," I reply. "He hired me to decorate his house for Christmas since this is his first year with Piper, and now we're suddenly dating. I don't usually date clients, so I'm hesitant, but...the chemistry's there, you know?"

"Oh, I know all too well," she says, flashing a smile. "Nate and I used to work at the same firm. That's how we met. We had a no-fraternization policy, and we fought it for a long time, but you can't choose who you're meant for, you know? I was fired from the job, and then Nate quit, and we started our own company. We work with Reed and Elijah quite a bit, so when they invited us to come tonight, we were happy to be here. And now I'm extra happy we came because I got to see you, and I don't think I know you well enough yet."

"Well, we're not technically related at all, even by marriage," I remind her. "My sister's married to your cousin's brother."

"Family's family," she says, shrugging one shoulder. "That's just how it is. It's not always blood. Also, there will probably be a Christmas girls' night out happening soon. I'll keep you posted."

"Thanks."

"Ladies," Reed says as he passes me a fresh glass of champagne, "I'm sorry to interrupt, but I need to steal my date away."

"Have fun," Jules says, a smile on her face as she turns to Nate. "I think you should dance with me."

"My pleasure," Nate says.

"We have friends in common," I say with a smile as Reed leads me to a table. "I like that."

"I do, too," he says and kisses my hand, then holds out a chair for me at the table marked *reserved*. "I'd like to introduce you to Elijah, my partner."

"I've heard a lot about you," I say as I reach over to shake Elijah's hand. "It's nice to meet you."

"Likewise," he says and then shifts his gaze to Reed. "I, on the other hand, know very little about you."

"I hired Noel to decorate my house for the holidays," Reed says. "And the rest is none of your business."

"I'm Becca." A pretty blonde woman holds out her hand for mine.

"I'm Reed's assistant. And this is my boyfriend, Lon."

"Nice to meet you both."

"I didn't know you had a boyfriend," Reed says brightly and shakes Lon's hand.

"Now you do." Becca grins in return. "Reed's a slave-driver, but he's fair, and I *love* working for him. So he's stuck with me."

"I wouldn't remember much without Becca," Reed admits.

"I totally get it, I'm the same way with my assistant. And finding a good one isn't easy, so I'm glad you found a good fit with each other."

The conversation swirls around us, and I soak it all in. Elijah's here alone because he doesn't date much, and his assistant isn't here at all, which doesn't please him.

Clients dance and mingle.

The food is amazing.

The atmosphere is joyful.

I like Reed's colleagues and friends very much.

I wonder what would happen if I didn't? Would I decide not to see him anymore? Maybe.

"You're thinking way too hard," Reed says, for my ears only. His arm rests on the back of my chair, and he leans in to whisper in my ear. "In twenty minutes, we can leave."

"That will only be an hour that we've been here."

"Plenty of time," he insists. "Piper's staying with Elijah's mom tonight, and I finally get you all to myself. I'd like to sling you over my shoulder and go right now, but that might be frowned upon."

"You're such a caveman." I laugh and sip my champagne. This is only glass number two, but I'm starting to feel a happy buzz.

Which means I need to slow down because I want all my wits about me tonight. I have a feeling I'm not going to want to forget *anything* that Reed does to me this evening.

So I set my glass aside, finish my dinner of steak and salad, and before I know it, we're saying goodbye.

"You just ditched your work party early," I say in surprise. "Reed, you *own* the company. Shouldn't you be there until the end?"

"Elijah will cover for me," he says with confidence. "Besides, people will start leaving now that dinner's over anyway. It's not really a rager of a party."

"I like them."

"Who?"

"All of them. They're nice, and smart. And I can tell that they respect you very much."

"Thank you," Reed says and helps me into his car. "Do you mind if I take you to my house tonight? I know the condos are both closer, but I prefer the house, what with all of the beautiful lights and touches that you worked so hard on. Piper's at the sitter's until tomorrow morning."

Before he shuts the door, he leans in and presses his lips to my ear.

"And I want to watch the lights reflect off of your body as I make you quiver with desire."

I swallow hard. "I didn't exactly pack a bag," I say, but then shrug my shoulder. "But if you don't mind that I wear this dress again tomorrow, then I don't either."

He laughs and pulls out of the parking garage, headed toward the freeway. "I'm sure I have something you can lounge in tomorrow morning. Besides, for what I have planned tonight, you don't need any clothes."

"Am I that much of a sure thing?" I ask, teasing him, but he frowns and glances at me as he merges onto the freeway. "Nothing about you is a sure thing, and I'm sorry if I sounded crass. Frankly, if you simply want to watch Hallmark movies all night and snuggle, I'm fine with that, too. I mean, it'll kill me to keep my hands to myself, but I'll be okay. I mean that."

"I was teasing you."

"But you bring up a good point. I just assumed we were on the same page, but I need to make sure you feel the same way."

Rather than say anything, I simply tug my skirt up around my waist and shimmy out of my panties. I toss the lace into the backseat of Reed's Mercedes, hitch one stiletto-tipped foot onto the dash and reach down to touch myself.

"Don't wreck."

His hand tightens on the wheel. He hasn't even glanced my way.

So I keep playing with myself, settling back into the leather seat, enjoying the moment.

"After you kissed me on the couch the other night, and your finger *almost* made it here"—I gently brush my fingertip over my clit and suck in a quick breath—"I went home and did this, imagining it was you. I don't know if I've ever been as turned on as I was that night. You know how to kiss a girl, and more than that, you're good with your hands—"

"If you keep talking," he says, his jaw tight, "I will run us off the road."

I glance at the speedometer. He's going eighty.

"You're speeding."

"Fuck, yes, I'm speeding. I need to get you home so I can bury myself inside you for hours." He glances my way now, his eyes moving from my face to my hands, and then when he watches the road again, he reaches over and covers my hand with his. "Slower. I don't want you to make yourself come. That's my job."

Maybe this was a bad idea. I thought it sounded like harmless, sexy flirting when I started, but now the sound of his voice, so full of lust and wanting as he shows me how he wants me to touch myself, has me worked into a frenzy.

And he's barely touched me.

So I breathe. I close my eyes and breathe and let myself feel all of the sensations washing through me.

I also pray with everything in me that we're almost there. Because, good God, a girl can only take so much.

Finally, I feel him slow down and take the exit. A few seconds later, we pull into the garage.

Before I can blink, he says, "Wait for me."

I know what that means now. He's going to open the door and help me out. He's nothing if not chivalrous.

He opens the door and lifts me, his arms under my legs and behind my back, out of the car. He nudges the door closed with his foot and carries me into the house after fumbling with the doorknob.

I shove my hands into his hair and bury my nose in his neck, kissing and gently biting him there as he maneuvers us through the house.

"I'm going to drop you if you don't stop that," he warns, but I just smile and carry on, too lost in the scent of him, in the feel of his warm skin against my lips to stop now. He climbs the stairs, and finally, *finally*, he lowers me to his bed. "I had half a mind to take you in my car. I should have. But I want the first time to be sweeter, so I held back."

"I don't want you to ever hold back with me." I can't believe the words coming out of my mouth are so bold, brazen. Why am I so comfortable with this man? So at ease that being wanton in front of him comes so easily?

My skirt is still bunched up around my waist, and he wastes no time settling between my legs, nudging them apart with his broad shoulders as he stares down at me. "Jesus, Mary, and Joseph, you're beautiful, Noel."

And with that, he leans in to take his first taste. He laps at me, skimming over my lips and my clit. Touching me so gently, I feel as if I might explode from it.

The lights on the Christmas tree are the only illumination in the room as he works me over, holding my hands hostage at my waist. He's strong, so much stronger than I am, but I feel totally safe with him.

And when I arch my back and succumb to the strongest orgasm of my life, it's Reed that catches me when I fall back to Earth.

"I need you." His voice is a rasp as he tears at his clothes, then mine, leaving us bare. "I wanted to take my time, to go slow, but—"

"We have time," I assure him. "We're *making* time, remember?"

His lips tip into a smile as he links his fingers with mine, and with his gaze intense, he slowly eases inside of me, leaving me speechless.

"Fucking hell," he whispers and tips his forehead to mine. "Like a damn glove."

My hips move of their own accord, needing to feel the push and pull of him, the sweet slide of pleasure as it works its way from my core and through all of my extremities until the pressure builds again and, with a cry of delight, we both fall over the edge together.

Some minutes later, after we've caught our breath and I can finally see again, I look into Reed's eyes and see not just affection there, but love.

And if that won't make a girl's heart catch, I don't know what will. It's scary, and not a little overwhelming.

But it's also incredible.

He doesn't have to say the words, I can *see* them.

"Do you feel like we're moving too fast?" I ask him.

"No." He frowns and tugs me closer, kisses my nose. "Do you?"

"It doesn't *feel* too fast," I admit. "It just *is* fast, and I know that people will say—"

"I don't give a rat's ass what they say," he replies calmly. "Why does love have to work on any certain timeline? Why can't it just *be*? I took one look at Piper, and I knew that I loved her, that I'd never be the same after meeting her."

"That's sweet."

"Why should it be okay with her, my daughter, and not okay regarding a woman that I care about very much? We're not hurting anyone, including my daughter."

"No, you're right."

"So I'm going to say don't worry about the timeline. We're going at *our* pace, Noel, and no one else's."

"You're right about that, too." I sigh and lean in to him, enjoying him.

"Spend the weekend with us," Reed says, kissing my head. "Piper and I would enjoy that. And I'll talk to her, answer any questions she might have. I don't want any awkwardness to happen for anyone."

"I'll stay tomorrow, but I can't on Sunday. I have a family dinner to go to." I frown and look up at him. "Actually, why don't you and Piper come with me? It'll just be my sister, Joy, her husband, and my dad."

"Do you think it'll be okay with everyone?" he asks.

"I mean, I think they'll be surprised since I haven't told them that I'm dating anyone. But, yes, they'll be happy to meet you. My dad might ask some tough questions, though."

"He's a dad. That's his job." Reed smiles at me. "If you're okay with it, we are, too."

"Cool. I'll text them in the morning."

"In the meantime," Reed says as he rolls me onto my tummy and covers my back with kisses, "I still have nine hours alone with you, and I plan to make use of every single one of them."

"We'll be tired tomorrow," I warn him.

"I've been tired before, and never for such a good reason." He bites my ass, and it makes me squeal. "Did you know you have a birthmark, right here?"

"Yes." I giggle when he brushes his nose over it. "That tickles."

"I think I'll explore every inch of you now. With my tongue."

"Holy shit."

Chapter Seven

~Reed~

"Hey, Shannon," Noel says to the barista at Cherry Street Coffee House. It's the morning after the most incredible, mind-blowing sex of my life, and Noel was adamant that we stop for her favorite coffee before I took her home.

"Hey yourself," Shannon says and winks, then looks at me with curiosity. "Who's your friend?"

"This is Reed. Reed, Shannon. She owns the place, and she's an artist when it comes to coffee."

"Trust me, Noel has sung the praises of your café pretty much since I met her." I smile at the woman as her cheeks flush with pleasure.

"Noel's just addicted," Shannon says. "Now, what can I get you, Reed? I already know what Noel wants."

"I might come here a lot," Noel says as she laughs.

"I'll have what she's having," I reply. "And a cinnamon roll."

"Oh, me too," Noel says, nodding happily.

After paying our tab, I slip my hand into Noel's as we wait for our drinks to be made. Shannon loads two plates up with the sweet rolls, warms them up, and before long, we're carrying our breakfast to a small table in the corner.

Before diving into the pastry, I take a sip of my coffee and then look at Noel in surprise.

"Okay, now I know what I've been missing."

"Told you," she says, a smug smile tugging at her lips. "Best coffee in town. And we're in Seattle, so that's saying something. Also, I'm sure each of these drinks is about six hundred calories, but I don't care."

"Totally worth it," I agree and dig into my cinnamon roll, then groan louder than I'm proud of. "Jesus, I'll gain sixty pounds if I keep this up."

"Totally worth it, remember?" She winks, takes a bite of her roll, and licks her lips, and I'm immediately reminded of how those lips feel on my body.

On my dick, thanks to a fun session in the shower this morning.

And just like that, I want her again. I'll never get enough of her. I could have sex with this woman for the next sixty years, and it wouldn't be enough.

But it wasn't just the sex, which was mind-numbing. We *talked*. For hours. We discussed more about our families, and I talked about Piper. She explained why her new design firm means so much to her. It was the most physically and emotionally fulfilling night of my life.

It's been a week, and I'm in way over my head.

But I like it. Since Piper and now Noel have come into my life, I feel more alive than I ever have.

And I refuse to lose this feeling. I'm going to marry this woman. Holy shit, I'm the consummate bachelor, the man who swore he'd never be tied down, and here I am, sitting here planning to marry a woman I just met.

But nothing in my life, aside from Piper, has ever felt so right.

"You're frowning," Noel says. "Do you not like it after all? You can save it for Piper. I'm sure she'll love it."

"No, it's great." I reach over and squeeze her hand. "I was just thinking that I want to spend the day with you. I know you need to go home for a bit, and I need to go get my girl, but I'd still like for you to be with us today."

She sips her coffee. I love the way her pinky curves out as she holds her cup.

"I just need to change and freshen up, so by the time you get Piper and circle back this way, I'll be ready to go. What do you have in mind?"

"Actually, now that we're allowed back in our home, I'd like to spend the day just hanging out. We can watch movies or play board games. Read. Whatever you want. I know all of that probably sounds boring."

"Actually, a laidback day sounds good. But I'll have to bring my computer because I have a couple of things to finish up. It won't take me long, though. I can even do it while a movie plays or something."

"Perfect."

We finish our breakfast, bus our own table, and wave to Shannon as we walk back out into the cold. Winter seems to have decided to visit Seattle over the past couple of days, turning the damp air bitter and biting.

"You don't have to walk me home," Noel says, but I stick by her side, take her hand in mine, and push them both into my pocket.

"I'll walk you home."

"So chivalrous," she says.

We both sigh in relief once inside Noel's building.

"Which floor?" I ask inside the elevator.

"Twelve," she replies and leans her cheek on my biceps as the elevator climbs to her floor. "I thought I'd be more tired today. After all, I think we only slept for about two hours total."

"You're not tired?"

"No more than usual." We step off the elevator, and she leads me to her door. "But a relaxing day sounds great."

"Good." When her door is open, I poke my head in and smile. "This is gorgeous, just as I suspected. It suits you."

"Thank you. I'll give you a tour, if you like."

"Later. I have to go get Piper, and if you lead me to your bedroom, I won't be going anywhere. I already want you again."

I grip the lapels of her jacket and tug her close, lowering my mouth to hers. The kiss starts lazy and sweet and quickly escalates to hot and frantic.

"I better go," I whisper against her mouth. "But pack a bag because you're staying at my place tonight."

"Piper—"

"Will be fine." I kiss her once more and then let go while I still can. "I'll see you in about an hour."

She nods, and I turn to leave.

"Lock this door behind me, please."

"Yes, sir."

I laugh as she shuts the door, and wait until I hear the snick of the lock being turned.

The drive to Elijah's parents' place takes about thirty minutes from downtown. I've barely rung the bell when the door swings open, and my little girl, already in her coat and boots, smiles at me with excitement.

"You're finally here!" she exclaims, launching herself into my arms. "I waited all day."

"It's only ten," I remind her as I laugh and smile at Betty, Elijah's mom. "How did everything go?"

"Oh, she's an angel," Betty says. "We had a good time. She's just happy to see her daddy."

"I appreciate you keeping her."

"Any time. And I mean that." She smiles at Piper, who's laid her head on my shoulder. "Thanks for staying with us last night, sweet girl."

"You're welcome," Piper says, making me laugh again.

We say our goodbyes, and when we're headed back to the city, I glance at Piper in the rearview mirror.

"What do you think about spending the day with Noel?"

"Is she gonna babysit?"

"No, she's going to hang out with both of us."

"Oh, yay!"

"Before we pick her up, we should buy her some flowers."

I pull into the parking lot of a florist and help my daughter out of the car.

"Why?" Piper asks.

"Because that's what men do. They buy flowers for women they like."

"I like flowers," she says. "I'll help pick them out."

"I was hoping you'd say that," I reply and lead her to a glass case with bouquets already assembled and ready to be purchased. "What color do you think we should get?"

"Lellow," Piper says, pointing to a bouquet of yellow roses and sunflowers.

"Not pink? Or red?"

"Hmm." She looks as if she's thinking really hard as she examines all of the flowers. "I like the red ones with the pink."

"Red roses and pink lilies it is," I say. I pay for the blooms, and once we're settled in the car and headed to Noel's condo, I decide now is a good time to have a conversation with my daughter. "Do you like Noel, honey?"

"Yeah. She's pretty."

"Yes, she is."

She's absolutely gorgeous.

"Do you like it when Noel spends time with us?"

"Yeah."

"Would you like for Noel to spend even more time with us?"

Piper frowns. "I don't know."

She's four. Maybe she doesn't understand what I'm asking her.

"I think it would be nice if Noel was with us all the time. She could spend the night, and maybe, someday, she could live with us."

She seems to think it over. "Will I have to share my room?"

"No, honey, she'll share my room."

"Okay."

That easy? I decide to leave it be for now. I'm sure Piper will have questions as time passes, but for now, I know that she likes having Noel around, and that's the most important part.

I park in my parking garage, which happens to have easy access to Noel's building as well, then I help Piper out of the car, and we make our way upstairs.

"Do you want to carry the flowers?" I ask.

Piper nods and holds out her hands for the blooms. The bouquet is almost as big as she is.

Noel opens the door, looking fresh from another shower, and smiles down at Piper.

"These are for you!" my daughter announces.

"Well, thank you so much," Noel says and squats next to my daughter. She takes the flowers, sniffs them, and then kisses Piper on the cheek. "This is the best surprise ever."

"Dad says that girls like flowers."

"Well, this girl does. What about you?"

"I do, too. I picked them out."

"Thank you," Noel says again before standing and smiling at me. "And thank you, too."

"You're welcome," I reply and turn my head, waiting for my kiss. Noel chuckles, then kisses my cheek.

"I think I'll take these with me to your place, so we can all enjoy them."

"Good idea. Where's your bag?"

"On the chair," she says, pointing to the dining room. "I'm ready if you are."

"Let's go."

I'm more than ready to have both of my girls tucked into my house for the day. There's no other way I'd rather spend it.

"Oh, I talked to my sister after you left. And, well, long story short, you and Piper are invited to join us for family dinner tomorrow."

I watch her face closely as we stand in the elevator.

"Is that what *you* want?"

I can tell she's trying to school her features.

"Sure. I mean, I wouldn't invite you if I didn't want you there. They won't bite."

"I'd love to come."

Her body sags as if in relief.

I lean in and kiss her cheek. "We're on our own timeline. Don't forget that."

* * * *

"It's a pleasure to meet you, Larry." I shake the older man's hand, meeting his gaze.

"It's a surprise to meet you," Larry replies and then hugs his daughter. "But then again, Noel has always been full of surprises."

"Funny, Dad," Noel says, rolling her eyes.

"I'm Piper," my daughter says and holds out her hand to shake.

"Well, hello there, Piper," Larry says, bending over to smile at my daughter. "It's lovely to meet you. Why, you look just like your daddy."

"Yup," my daughter says, nodding. "You have a puppy!"

"This is Nancy," Noel says and scratches the one-eyed bulldog behind the ear. "She used to belong to my sister, Joy, but Nancy loves being here with my dad."

"And who wouldn't?"

We glance over to see a man and a woman walk out of the kitchen.

"I'm Jase," the man says.

"And I'm Joy, the other daughter. You know, the selfless one who gave up her dog for her daddy."

"She's also humble," Jase says with a laugh.

Noel takes our jackets and hangs them up in a hall closet, and we move into the living space.

"Your home is lovely," I say and turn to Noel. "Did you grow up here?"

"We did," she says and grins. "Dad bought the house shortly after I was born, and we've been here ever since."

"I love that," I say as I take a seat in the living room. Piper and Nancy are getting acquainted, playing nearby. "It's what I want for Piper, as well. That's why I bought the house as soon as she came to live with me."

"She hasn't always been with you?" Larry asks.

"No, sir." I take a moment to fill Noel's family in on how Piper came to be with me and when. "So both of our lives were turned on their ear, but I think we're coming through it just fine."

"It looks that way to me," Joy says, a soft smile on her lips. "Noel, would you please help me in the kitchen?"

"Is that code for leave Reed alone to fend for himself with Jase and Daddy?" Noel asks.

"No, it's code for I want all the details, so come with me right now."

Noel laughs and looks over at me. "Are you good here?"

"I'm great."

"Okay, then. Come on, Piper, the girls are going into the kitchen. But I want you to know, right now, that a woman's place is *not* always in the kitchen, okay? You can be whatever you want to be."

"I want to be a princess!" Piper exclaims as she follows Noel and Joy into the kitchen, Nancy hurrying along behind them. Once the swinging door shuts, I look at the two men sitting across from me.

"I guess it's a good thing that I never remodeled that kitchen like the girls always pestered me to, for moments like this one." Larry crosses one ankle over the other knee and levels his gaze on me. "Tell me about yourself, Reed."

I'm in the most important interview of my life. I want to make a good impression. I want Piper and me to belong here.

Because the woman I love loves them. And I'm old enough to know that when you fall in love with a person and want them to be your family, you automatically get their family as well.

"I'm from Issaquah," I begin and tell Larry and Jase about my family. My business. My daughter.

"I've heard of your firm," Jase says. "I'm the chief of cardiothoracic surgery at Seattle General. Several of my colleagues are your clients."

"I can't confirm or deny that," I say, smiling.

"I'll be honest," Larry says, leaning forward, "I am impressed by your resume, and I like your sweet daughter very much. You seem like a nice man. But I want to know what your intentions are with *my* daughter."

"I think they just started dating," Jase reminds him. "It might be early days for this conversation."

"I have eyes in my head," Larry says. "And I'm looking at a man in love."

"You're not wrong." I brace my elbows on my knees and lean forward, looking Larry right in the eyes. "I'm in love with her. And, yes, it's early days, but I don't care. I plan to have Noel in my life for as long as I'm breathing, if she'll have me. I know it's asking a lot because I have a child. It's a big commitment, but I'm going to ask it of her anyway because the thought of being without her is devastating."

"You hardly know her," Larry points out. "What happens when she spends too much money on one of those shopping sprees she enjoys?"

"With all due respect, sir, your daughter is incredibly successful. She can buy whatever she wants, whenever she wants."

"Not a very responsible way of thinking for a financial planner," Larry says.

"Noel doesn't give the impression of an irresponsible woman. She owns her home, has a nice car, a successful business. She takes care of things, and I don't need to see her bank balance to know that. I'm also successful, and not that she would need me to, but I'll always take care of my family, Mr. Thompson."

"I like you," Jase says, leaning back in his seat with a grin. "Our little Noel finally met her match."

"*Your* little Noel?"

"I've known her since she was a kid," he says. "And I can tell you, she's never met anyone as good for her as you are."

"That we know of," Larry says and sighs. "I'm being difficult. I like you, too. But she's my baby, and I'm going to just say, here and now, that if you hurt her, I'll hurt you."

"Understood," I say immediately. "I have a daughter, sir. I'm not here to hurt anyone. I'm here because I can't stay away from Noel."

"Dinner's ready," Joy calls as she and Noel begin setting platters and bowls on the table, bustling in and out of the kitchen.

"And now that you've drilled poor Reed, we're going to drill you about your date last night," Noel adds with a satisfied grin as she helps Piper get settled at the table, dishing up her plate.

In a matter of days, she's become as easy and comfortable with Piper as I am.

"Now, there's no need to go into that," Larry says.

"Oh, there's every need," Joy says as she takes a seat. "Tell us everything."

Chapter Eight

~Noel~

"Dad, we want to know *everything*," I inform my father before eating a bite of lemon chicken. This whole visit has been disconcerting. Not only did I introduce Reed and Piper to my family, but as I gaze around the house, I see that Dad has started to clear some of our mom's things away.

After she passed, he left everything exactly the way it was. There was even a dust rag on the mantel. He refused to change anything.

But the dust rag is now gone, and he bought new kitchen towels. It doesn't sound like a big thing, but for our dad, it's *huge*.

"Her name is Martha, and I met her at the senior center. She kicked my ass at poker."

Joy and I share a glance and then laugh. Mom always hated when Dad went out for poker night.

Now he's met a woman that can beat him!

"And how did the date go?" Jase asks.

"Fairly well, I suppose. I haven't been out on a date in forty years." He sighs and sets his fork down. "Now, I don't want you girls to think that I'm trying to replace your mother or anything like that."

"Dad," Joy says, reaching over to pat his shoulder, "we're all adults here. Trust me, we know how much you love and miss Mom. Replacing her isn't what this is."

"It's just nice to have a conversation with someone who answers me," Dad says with a grin. "Nancy's a good listener, but not a great conversationalist."

"I'm happy for you, Dad," I say. "When do we get to meet her?"

"Well, I guess Sunday dinners are for introducing new people," Dad says, smiling at Reed. "How about next Sunday?"

"I'm on call," Joy says, a frown turning down her lips. "We can plan it, but if there's an emergency at the clinic, I'll duck out."

"We can do it in two weeks, then," Dad says and nods.

"Can I come?" Piper asks, speaking for the first time. She's been watching us with wide, brown eyes, soaking in the conversation.

"Well, I sure hope you will," Dad says. "I'll need someone to protect me from these two."

He points to Joy and me, and Piper giggles.

"I'm just a little girl!"

Reed reaches for my hand under the table and gives it a squeeze. I was so nervous about bringing them today, but they're both fitting in as if they've been coming to family dinners for years.

I can't help but wonder when the other shoe will drop. Is this too good to be true?

* * * *

It's Wednesday afternoon, and I haven't seen Reed since Sunday evening. Since I took the past few weekends off, and because I squeezed Reed's project into my schedule, I'm now chained to my desk, buried in work.

Ali's been working late with me. I think I can almost see the light at the end of this tunnel. Finally.

"Hey, Noel, your four o'clock is here," Ali says, poking her head in my office.

"Great, thanks."

Alex Fisher and I go way back. He lived in our neighborhood growing up, and we played together almost every day. He's like a brother to me.

And he recently hired me to decorate his new office space in

Tacoma.

"Hey, girl," he says, walking around my desk to give me a hug. "How's it going?"

"Pretty good, actually." He sits on the other side of my desk. "Sorry I had to postpone our meeting."

"No biggie. I can't wait to see what you've done with it."

We spend the next hour looking at 3-D images of his office with different options for seating, desks, colors, and other details.

Finally, once he's decided on the option he likes the best, we stand and stretch.

"It's going to be gorgeous," Alex says, smiling. "You're good at what you do."

Yes, I am.

"Thank you."

"You know, Libby and I broke up a couple of months ago."

"I hadn't heard. I'm sorry to hear that. I figured you two would tie the knot."

"Yeah, well." He shrugs a shoulder, and then a smile spreads slowly over his face, and I realize that he's about to come on to me.

Well, shit.

"Don't look at me like that, Alex."

"Noel, I think we'd be good together."

"You're on the rebound, that's all. Besides, you're a client, and more importantly, you're my *friend*. Let's not screw that up, okay?"

"Yeah." He sighs and looks sad, and I can't help but feel bad for him. So I walk to him and give him a hug.

"Everything's going to work out," I assure him.

"You can't blame a guy for trying, right?"

I laugh and kiss his cheek.

"What the fuck is this?"

I pull away from Alex and scowl at a very angry Reed, who's currently lurking in my doorway. His hands are fisted at his sides, and he's glaring daggers at both Alex and me.

"I'm Alex, and I'm just leaving."

Without an apology, Alex kisses my cheek, walks past Reed, and saunters out of my office.

Reed steps inside and closes the door behind him.

"Who the hell is that?"

"A childhood friend." I cross my arms over my chest. "And a client."

"He had his hands on you."

"He was *hugging* me. Or, rather, I was hugging him. Because he recently broke up with his girlfriend, and he's sad."

"Did he come on to you?"

I tip my head to the side, watching as Reed's jaw tics. "Half-heartedly. I shut him down. What the hell? Are you jealous, Reed?"

"You bet your ass I'm jealous."

I laugh and shake my head, then return to my spot behind my desk.

"I don't find this funny."

"I think it's hilarious. If you can walk into this room and think that I was about to get it on with Alex, you're blind. And if you can't see what I feel for you every time I look at you, well, then you're blind *and* dumb."

He runs his hand through his hair in agitation.

"I wasn't expecting you today," I say.

"I haven't seen you in *days*." He walks to me, but I hold a hand up.

"You don't get to touch me right now. I'm pissed. I didn't do anything wrong."

"You kissed him."

"On the cheek."

"I didn't like it." He sighs, and I can see the fatigue on his face. I don't say no when he crosses to me and lifts me out of the chair, then sits and cradles me. "I haven't touched you. I missed you."

"Okay, that's sweet." I brush my fingers through his disheveled hair. "I missed you, too. Even if you act like a caveman."

"Caveman?" He lifts a brow and presses his lips to my ear. "I'm about to fuck you on your desk, Noel. How do you feel about that?"

My nipples immediately pucker. My core tightens.

"Apparently, I feel pretty good about it. But Ali's on the other side of that door."

"We'll be quiet."

He lifts me again and plants my ass on my desk. He nudges my legs apart, cradles my face, and kisses me. Deeply, as if he's starving for me.

As if he can't get enough of me.

One hand drifts down my chest, my thigh, and moves under my skirt. He nudges the edge of my panties aside and easily slips that magical finger into my wetness.

"Jesus, you're slick," he whispers.

"Even though you pissed me off, that whole jealous thing kind of turned me on."

His brown eyes are on fire. "Yeah?"

"Oh, yeah. Honestly, if I was the one to walk in on you with a woman, I would have ripped her hair out."

He laughs and then slips that wet finger into his own mouth to suck it clean.

Good God, he's sexy.

He surprises me by pulling me off the desk, turning me away from him, and pushing me again, face-down this time. He gathers my skirt up around my waist, and when my ass is bare, he gives it a light slap.

I moan. I can hear the zipper of his pants give way, and the next thing I know, he's dragging the tip of his cock up and down over my wet folds.

I want him so badly, I can't think straight.

"Don't make any noise," he warns me before sliding inside me, one amazing inch at a time until he's seated balls-deep.

He leans down, his front pressed to my back, and kisses my neck. "I've been thinking of this, and little else, for days. Do you have any idea how badly I want you? It's constant, Noel."

He's whispering, making as little noise as possible while he moves in small motions, rubbing the root of his dick against my core.

"This, all of this, is mine, do you understand?"

"Hell, yes," I mutter. "Faster, Reed."

"You want more?"

I nod, not caring in the least that I'm wrinkling all the papers I've worked hard on today. Or that I'm sprawled out, ass up, over my desk, practically begging Reed to fuck the hell out of me.

I wasn't lying, I *did* miss him.

Missed this.

He doesn't disappoint. He moves faster, pushes harder. I have to cover my mouth with my hand to keep from crying out, it feels so damn amazing.

With another slap on my ass, Reed grips my hips tightly and pulses against me, buried deeply as he falls over the edge, taking me with him.

My legs have never shaken like this before.

Good God, Reed's ruined me for all other men.

He slips out of me, tugs my skirt back down, and when I turn around, he's smiling down at me like the cat that ate the canary.

"You look awfully pleased with yourself."

"I'm pleased with both of us." He kisses me softly. "Did I hurt you?"

"Nope, you can do that pretty much any time."

There's a knock on my door, but Ali doesn't open it.

"Yes?" I call.

"I'm leaving for the night," she calls back. "See you tomorrow!"

"Thanks, Ali."

My eyes are still pinned to Reed's.

"She totally heard us," I inform him. His lips twitch.

"How do you know?"

"I've worked with Ali for five years. I could hear the smile in her voice, and she didn't open the door. She *always* opens the door."

"Well. She's an adult woman. She'll recover."

"I'll have to add counseling to her benefits package."

Reed chuckles and kisses my forehead. "Come home with me tonight."

"I can't. I *want* to, trust me, but I just can't tonight. I've been out of my office too much lately, and I have to catch up because I'd like to take weekends off to be with you and Piper."

He sighs, but he doesn't give me a guilt trip or try to talk me into it. He just kisses my forehead again and pulls me in for a big, strong hug.

"Okay. I brought my laptop. Do you mind if I work for a bit with you?"

I lean back and frown. "Where's Piper?"

"One of her classmates asked if she could have a play date tonight. I have a couple hours until I pick her up."

"In that case, absolutely. You're welcome to work with me."

I didn't even notice that he had a briefcase in his hand when he arrived. I just saw *him*.

When we settle in to work, Reed looks at me over his laptop. "I apologize for earlier, Noel. For jumping to conclusions when I saw you hug that other guy. It was uncalled for."

"Thank you for that. You don't have anything to worry about, Reed. I'm not interested in Alex or anyone else, for that matter."

We order in dinner and sit in companionable silence as we both work on projects and chew on our Chinese food.

I've never been as comfortable with anyone as I am with Reed.

I've never *loved* anyone the way I love him.

Chapter Nine

~Noel~

It's been a *fast* week. I can't believe it's Friday. I'm exhausted, but if all goes well today, I'll be all caught up and free to take the weekend off with my two favorite people.

I haven't seen Reed since Wednesday when he surprised me at the office. And I haven't seen Piper since Sunday. We've been FaceTiming every evening, but it's not the same.

Reed told me last night that Piper's been fussier than normal, and when he asked her why, she said she misses me.

Yes, that melted my heart.

If you'd asked me a month ago if I'd ever consider dating a single dad, I would have said absolutely not. I'm not convinced I want to be a parent, or I *wasn't* anyway. And not because I don't like kids, but because my lifestyle is very...adult. I live in a condo in the city. I work long hours. I barely see my sister and dad. I don't know how I'd find time for children.

And that's still a concern for me. But I know that I'm in love with Reed and Piper, and I miss them every day that I don't see them.

So I'm ready to get through this day and get to Reed's house this evening.

With a spring in my step, I walk around the corner to Cherry Street

Coffee House and stop short when I walk inside and see who's at the counter.

"What are you doing here?" I ask as I approach.

"Making time," Reed says with a smile. He passes me my coffee and leans in to kiss my lips. "I wanted to see you this morning."

"Thank you." I have butterflies. Not little ones, but huge, gigantic butterflies. He made it into the city early, came to my favorite spot where he knew he'd catch me, and bought my coffee.

Is it any wonder I'm in love with him?

He leads me to our table in the corner, but before I can follow him, Shannon waves to catch my attention and then mouths *I REALLY LIKE HIM.*

I respond with ME TOO! And follow my man to our seats.

"How are you this morning?" I ask before taking a sip.

"Tired. Ready for the weekend. How are you?"

"The same." I grin as he reaches over to link his fingers with mine. "But as of this afternoon, I'll be all caught up and can enjoy the weekend. Do we have plans?"

"I thought it would be fun to take Piper to look at Christmas lights. Not that there are many homes as beautiful as mine, thanks to you, but it might be a good time."

"I'm game. I love doing that. We used to do it all the time when we were kids."

"We did, too."

"Did you know the botanical gardens in Bellevue have a fantastic holiday lights display?"

"I think I heard that," he says. "Let's do that, too."

"Sounds good."

Reed's phone rings, and he pulls it out of his jacket to answer. He frowns when he looks at the caller ID.

"Hello? Yes. That's good news." His face relaxes but then tightens again as the person keeps talking. "You're kidding. When? I'll be there."

He hangs up, tosses the phone onto the table, and runs his hand down his face.

"What's wrong?"

"That was Piper's social worker. The one who brought her to me in the first place. She has news."

I reach over to take his hand. "What's the news?"

"It seems Piper's maternal grandparents have surfaced. And they want to meet her."

"I'm confused."

"That makes two of us." He drinks his coffee. "I was told that Vanessa had no immediate family, but it turns out they were just estranged. So the grandparents want Piper."

His brown eyes hold mine.

"What if they want to take her away from me?"

"Not gonna happen."

He licks his lips. The confident man I know is nervous.

"It's literally *not* going to happen, Reed."

"You're right," he says, nodding as he forces a smile. "It's just a formality. I guess we'll find out Monday, won't we? I'll call my attorney as soon as I get to the office."

"I can take off work today and—"

"No, don't be ridiculous," he interrupts. "You're right, this is nothing. I'll see you this evening. Just come over after you're finished at work."

"Okay. If you need me before then, just call."

We stand and toss our empty cups into the recycling.

"I'm fine." He kisses my temple. "Thank you. See you soon."

He hurries out, and I'm left to frown after him. He says everything's fine, but it's not. He shut down, went a little cold on me. I know this new development has him unsettled.

And we both have to get to work.

But I'm worried about him.

I'll do my best to wrap things up early so I can get over to Reed's as soon as possible.

* * * *

"Hello?"

I still have the codes to Reed's house, so I walk inside and frown when I don't see or hear anyone. It's just past two in the afternoon. I was a maniac at my desk today.

I think I scared Alison.

The thought of that makes me laugh. Actually, nothing scares Alison.

Okay, maybe the thought of her boss getting it on behind a closed door startled her.

I'm still smiling at the thought when I hear the garage door open. Reed and Piper must just be getting home.

"Noel!" Piper calls as she hurries into the house. She drops her unicorn backpack and runs to me, arms outstretched for a hug. "You're here!"

"I'm here," I agree and kneel so I can wrap my arms around her and smooch her cheek. "I get to spend the whole weekend with you. How are you, baby girl?"

"Good. My friend Abby got a new puppy, and she got to bring it to class for us to see. It's so cute!"

"I bet it is."

"She's been begging *me* for a puppy since I picked her up," Reed says as I stand and offer him a hug as well. "I'm glad you're here."

"Me, too. I finished up early and came right over."

"Are we gonna watch movies this weekend?" Piper asks.

"I think we will," Reed replies. "But after dinner, we're going to take a drive to see some pretty lights. What do you think about that?"

"I like Christmas lights," Piper says. "Can I have chicken stwips for dinner?"

"I picked some up," I confirm, earning a surprised look from Reed. "I grabbed a few groceries on my way. I'm going to cook tonight, if that's okay."

"That's perfect," he says. He looks tired, and his eyes still look strained. "You're my hero today."

"I'm just a hungry girl," I reply with a laugh and walk out to my car to retrieve the bags of groceries. Reed and Piper follow, and I pass Piper a bag of bread but pretend it's really heavy. "Be careful with this one. You need lots of muscles to carry it."

Piper giggles. "It's not heavy."

"Maybe you're just strong."

Piper helps me unpack the groceries, and I make us a snack of cheese and crackers with a sliced apple and some grapes as I get to work on getting dinner in the oven. We sing songs and dance around the kitchen, having our own little party while I work.

"Can I have the iPad?" Piper asks. This is the usual time of day that the little girl gets to have some screen time, so I set it up for her and then go in search of Reed.

But he's not in the house.

I look again in his bedroom, his office, but he's nowhere to be found.

"He would have told me if he was leaving the house," I murmur as I glance outside and see Reed sitting on a chair, watching the Sound below.

I check on Piper real quick. "Honey, I'm going to step outside for just a minute, okay? I'll be right back."

She doesn't even look up when she says, "Okay."

I walk outside, pulling my cardigan around me against the cold air. Reed sits, one ankle balanced on the other knee, his fingers steepled under his chin.

He's clearly deep in thought.

"Penny for your thoughts," I say as I nudge his leg down so I can climb into his lap.

"I'm just zoning out."

I kiss his jaw, his neck, and then whisper in his ear, "Bullshit."

His arms tighten around me. "Work was busy today. I need to hire a nanny. I just have a lot on my mind."

"Okay." I don't like that he's pulled back a bit, but I understand stress, and sometimes you just need someone to listen. To hug you and be there with you.

So I don't push.

"What's Piper up to?"

"She's watching the iPad. Dinner's in the oven. When I went to look for you, I worried when I couldn't find you."

"Sorry. I just wanted some fresh air."

"It's cold out here."

"I'm not so cold with you on my lap. You're a nice blanket."

I laugh and bury my face in his neck. "I'm happy to help."

Chapter Ten

~Reed~

"Which lights did you like best?" I ask my daughter. We went to the botanical gardens today, and stayed past dark so we could see all of the pretty light displays. Piper couldn't get enough of it.

"I liked the frogs." She yawns and nestles her bunny under her chin. I'm tucking her in for the night. We already read through three holiday books, and I should kiss her and go, but I'm feeling extra clingy when it comes to my daughter this weekend.

It's been a rough few days.

That phone call on Friday fucked me up, big time.

"The frogs had Santa hats on," I say, smiling. "Do you want me to turn your tree off tonight?"

"No, I like the lights." She yawns again. "I can see better when I have to tinkle."

I make a mental note to add a couple nightlights to her bedroom and bathroom after we take down the Christmas decorations.

"Okay, baby. I love you. You know that, right?"

Her eyes are closed as she nods her head.

God, I love her so much, my heart aches with it.

I kiss her forehead and then walk across the hall to where Noel is packing her overnight bag.

"It's only Saturday night."

"I know," she says and shrugs. "I'm not leaving, I'm just organizing. These are dirty clothes."

"You can wash them here. Hell, I'll wash them tomorrow when I do mine and Piper's laundry."

"You don't have to do that."

I cover her hand with mine, stopping her movements. "Look at me."

She complies, but her eyes are full of tears.

"Baby, what's wrong?"

"I've been asking you the same thing for two days," she says and wipes a tear away in frustration. "I get that you're under stress, and I'm guessing your meeting on Monday has messed with your head, but you've withdrawn from me, and I don't know what to do. I've been understanding, attentive, all of the things I know to do. But you won't talk to me, and I feel like you're pushing me away, and I hate it."

"Whoa." I pull her to me, pick her up, and take us over to the sofa in the corner. I sit with her in my arms and brush a strand of hair off her cheek. "I'm not pushing you away. At least, that's not what I mean to do."

"You *have* to talk to me, Reed. Because the past couple of days has me feeling insecure, and that's not what I want in a relationship. Don't brush me off when I ask what's wrong."

"You're right." I sigh and kiss her temple, breathing her in. "It's not fair to you to do that. I apologize, and I'll do my best not to do it again in the future. Just call me out on it if I fuck up, okay?"

"Okay. I can do that. Now, talk to me."

She drags her fingertips down my cheek. That I've made Noel feel anything but loved and cared for tears me up inside.

She deserves so much more than that.

"I'm scared out of my mind," I admit and swallow hard. "Piper's only been with me for a few months, but she's *mine*, you know? I don't think I could love her more than I do. And the thought that some strangers could come in and just snatch her out of my hands has me debilitated with fear."

"Reed," she says with a sigh. "They can't do that. I don't know all of the ins and outs of the law here, but Shannon at Cherry Street has a foster daughter, and I've learned a little bit about the process from her.

Yes, sometimes, the court will give grandparents rights to a child, but Reed, you're her father. You've provided a wonderful home for her, she's loved and respected. There's no way a judge would pull her out of your home to give her to people she's never even *met* before. They'd only do that if she were in foster care."

"I know that. I spent the morning researching and making some calls to a couple of clients who happen to be attorneys, not to mention, my own attorney spent an hour on the phone with me. But, Noel, what if something crazy happens? What if the judge is stupid, or the grandparents sue me for custody of her?"

"Then we fight it," she says fiercely and cups my face in her hands, her eyes pinned to mine. "We fight it with everything we've got because the only place in the world that Piper belongs is right here, in this house, with you."

"You said *we*."

"Hell, yes I said we. And those people will know, without a shadow of a doubt, when we walk into that office on Monday that if they think they're going to try to take Piper from us, they'll have the biggest fight of their lives on their hands."

"Wait." I tip my forehead against hers, absorbing her strength. The fierceness in her face right now is astounding. "You're coming with me?"

"Of course." She frowns. "I mean, I was planning to. If you'd rather I not, I understand. It's really none of my business."

"Stop talking." I tilt her chin up and kiss her silly. "Of course it's your business. It just didn't occur to me that you'd want to go with me, but I want nothing more in the world than to have you by my side."

"Then I'll go." She smiles happily. "It hurts my heart that you've been worrying so much about this, Reed. You're not going to lose your daughter. There's just no way."

"I love you." The words are out of my mouth before I can stop them. But, damn it, I'm not sorry.

I *do* love her, and it's about time I told her.

"And not just for this, but for a million reasons. Thank you, so much, for everything you do for us, and for all the ways you show me what it means to have a partner."

Her eyes well with tears again.

"Don't cry."

"I love you, too," she says, her chin quivering. "I love you both."

* * * *

"Thank you for meeting with us," Ms. Hale says as she greets Noel and me at her office Monday morning.

Sunday was more relaxed, but the worry hasn't totally left me, despite Noel's pep talk the other night.

I'm ready to get this meeting over with so we can move on with our lives.

"This is Noel Thompson, and she'll be with me today," I reply, leaving no room for argument.

"Hello," Noel says. We're led to a conference room where an older couple already sits. They're both gray-haired but look to be in good health.

"I'm Reed Taylor," I announce, taking charge of the room. "And this is Noel Thompson, the love of my life."

Noel gasps and squeezes my hand, then nods at the couple.

"I'm Les, and this is my wife, Betsy." They both shake our hands, and then we all sit. Les takes a deep breath. The other man looks tired. "I want to tell you, first and foremost, that we're not here to disrupt our granddaughter's life. I looked into you, Reed, and I can see that you're a successful man."

"But we want to make sure that her emotional needs are met as well," Betsy adds and dabs at a tear. "And we'd like to meet her."

"I have some questions," I reply, not agreeing or disagreeing to Betsy's request. "Why were you estranged from Vanessa?"

"Oh." Betsy sighs and shakes her head slowly. "We always had a tough relationship with our daughter. And not for the usual reasons. There were no drugs or lifestyle decisions that drove a wedge between us."

"Vanessa was staunchly independent," Les says, folding his hands. "From a young age, she wanted to do things alone. She never told us about school functions that we should attend, like games or meetings."

"I had to stay in touch with her teachers," Betsy says. "She was private, and I guess you could say that we just never bonded with her."

"Was she an only child?" Noel asks.

"Yes, and I regret that," Betsy admits. "Maybe if we'd had more children, she would have felt differently about family. She left for college and rarely came home to visit. And the more we asked, the less she'd cooperate."

"We loved our daughter," Les says. "And I believe she loved us, in the only way she knew how."

"I can't believe she didn't even tell you she had Piper. Or that she was sick."

"Well, not telling us about her daughter came as quite a surprise," Betsy says, her voice quivering. "But her illness? No. I'm not surprised. She just didn't reach out about things like that. I wish she had told us so we could have been with her."

"But she wouldn't have wanted that either," Les adds and reaches for his wife's hand.

"None of us are bad people," Betsy insists. "Just different. And now that we know we have a granddaughter, we'd like the chance to get to know her."

"Are you planning to file for custody?" Noel asks, her voice strong.

Les and Betsy look at each other in surprise.

"No," Les says. "We're not young people. We raised our family. But this is the only chance we have at being grandparents."

"We live in Florida," Betsy adds. "So we can't see Piper often, but we'd like to make the trip a few times a year. Perhaps we can spend a holiday or two with you."

Ms. Hale clears her throat. "If need be, Les and Betsy can petition the court for visitation rights. Or you can simply make that decision among yourselves, and not involve the court at all."

I take a deep breath and sit back in the chair, watching the older couple before me. Vanessa looked so much like her mother. I don't know what her reasons were for not having a relationship with her parents, but I don't have the heart to keep Piper away from them.

If I discover something is off later, we can always adjust things.

And they won't take her by themselves. At least, not for a long time.

"There's no need to involve the court," I say at last. Betsy dissolves into tears, and Les nods his head.

"Thank you," he says.

"How long are you in town?"

"Only for a couple of days," Betsy says. "Do you think we can meet her before we go? We brought her some Christmas gifts, and I'd just love to see her."

"We can arrange that," Noel says and smiles. "I'm sure she'll love the idea of having more people in her life to love and to love her."

We exchange phone numbers and agree to meet the following afternoon.

Once in the car, I sigh and just stare straight ahead.

"You were right," I say at last.

"About which part?"

"That I had no reason to worry."

She reaches for my hand. "You're a daddy, Reed. Worrying is going to be part of your daily life for the next hundred years."

"As long as I have you to remind me that everything's okay, I'll be just fine."

"Everything's okay," she says with a smile. "I promise."

Epilogue

Three Months Later

~Noel~

"I don't know what to do with this." I sit on my haunches in the middle of my office in my condo and sigh. I'm sweaty. I'm tired.

My muscles hurt.

Who would have thought that moving was so freaking *exhausting*?

Reed offered to hire movers for me, but I really needed to go through everything myself. Purge what I don't need, and safely pack what I'm taking with me to his house.

Our house.

The house with the killer view of Puget Sound.

He's even letting me redecorate the whole place, which is awesome, considering I can't stand that stark white anymore.

"Do you use it?" Reed asks, pointing to the box in my hands.

"No, but someone gave it to me. So I should keep it, right?"

"Who gave it to you?"

"I have no idea."

He pauses in packing my paperbacks and laughs at me. "Honey, I think if you can't remember who gave it to you, and you don't use it anymore, you can get rid of it."

"Okay." I blow a piece of hair out of my face and reach for the next thing. "I'm donating almost everything in here. All I really use is my laptop and sketchpads."

"That's not surprising," he says. "Sidebar. Is this book as dirty as it looks from the cover?"

I glance over to see what he's holding, then smile. "Dirtier."

"Maybe I should start reading *you* bedtime stories," he says.

"That could be interesting." I laugh and stand, stretching and pushing against my aching lower back. "I wasn't made for manual labor. This is torture."

"I offered—"

"Yeah, yeah." I wave him off. "Moving is hard. Maybe I'll just keep this place and move a little at a time each day until it's empty."

"No way," he says as he follows me out of the office to my kitchen. I pull a bottle of water out of the fridge and pass it to him, then take another out for myself. "I'm excited to have you in *my* bed every single night. This whole back and forth game we've been playing for the past few months is getting old."

"We are putting a lot of miles on our cars," I concede. "And your condo already sold, so we might as well sell this one, too."

"You haven't actually slept here since just after Christmas," he reminds me. "Sell it and invest the money you'll make."

"You're always so practical." I push up on my toes to kiss his chin. "It's just one of the million reasons I love you."

"I love you, too."

"Come on, we better get this done."

"I have something to do first," he says, making me frown.

"We have to pick up Piper in an hour, and I still have to—"

"Stop talking," he says with a laugh and leads me to the couch. We sit, and he suddenly looks nervous.

What's wrong now?

"I've been thinking," he says.

"If you've changed your mind about me moving in with you, I might have to smack you, because we've already moved half my stuff."

"No." He takes my left hand in his and kisses my knuckles. "No, you're stuck with me until the end of time, Noel."

"Okay."

"I've been thinking that I want to make it more official, though. I love you. So much that sometimes it hurts. You've brought peace, comfort, and love to my house, and I'm forever grateful. Piper adores you."

"Did I tell you she asked me when she could call me Mommy?"

"She wasn't supposed to say anything," he mutters. "Marry us."

He pulls a ring out of his jeans' pocket. The diamond sparkles in the light.

"Marry us and make us the happiest two people in the world."

"Three," I reply. "We'll be the happiest three people in the world."

"Until we have more babies," he murmurs as he kisses me. "Is that a yes?"

"Yes! Oh my gosh, yes."

He buries his face in my neck, placing a kiss in that spot that makes me weak in the knees, and takes a deep breath.

"Are you okay?" I ask him.

"I knew I was nervous, and excited, and *ready* to ask you to be mine forever," he says as he pulls back to look me in the eyes. "But the wonder I feel every time I'm with you? It's unlike anything else I've ever felt in my life."

I smile and lean into him. I know we need to work a little more, and Piper will be expecting us soon. But for right now, I want to revel in this moment with him, and share in the wonder of our love for each other.

* * * *

Also from 1001 Dark Nights and Kristen Proby, discover Shine With Me, Soaring With Fallon, Tempting Brooke, No Reservations, Easy With You, and Easy For Keeps.

Sign up for the 1001 Dark Nights Newsletter
and be entered to win a Tiffany Key necklace.

There's a contest every month!

Go to www.1001DarkNights.com to subscribe.

**As a bonus, all subscribers can download
FIVE FREE exclusive books!**

Discover 1001 Dark Nights Collection Six

Go to www.1001DarkNights.com to subscribe

DRAGON CLAIMED by Donna Grant
A Dark Kings Novella

ASHES TO INK by Carrie Ann Ryan
A Montgomery Ink: Colorado Springs Novella

ENSNARED by Elisabeth Naughton
An Eternal Guardians Novella

EVERMORE by Corinne Michaels
A Salvation Series Novella

VENGEANCE by Rebecca Zanetti
A Dark Protectors/Rebels Novella

ELI'S TRIUMPH by Joanna Wylde
A Reapers MC Novella

CIPHER by Larissa Ione
A Demonica Underworld Novella

RESCUING MACIE by Susan Stoker
A Delta Force Heroes Novella

ENCHANTED by Lexi Blake
A Masters and Mercenaries Novella

TAKE THE BRIDE by Carly Phillips
A Knight Brothers Novella

INDULGE ME by J. Kenner
A Stark Ever After Novella

THE KING by Jennifer L. Armentrout
A Wicked Novella

Discover More Kristen Proby

Shine With Me: A With Me in Seattle Novella
Coming November 10, 2020

Sabrina Harrison *hates* being famous. She walked away from show business, from the flashing bulbs and prying eyes years ago, and is happy in her rural Oregon home, dedicating her life to her non-profit.

Until Hollywood calls, offering her the role of a lifetime. In more than ten years, she's never felt the pull to return to the business that shunned her, but this role is everything Sabrina's ever longed for.

Now she has to get in shape for it.

Benjamin Demarco's gym, Sound Fitness, continues making a name for itself in Seattle. And now, he finds himself with the task of training Sabrina, getting her in shape for the role of her life. He's trained hundreds of women. This is his job. So why does he suddenly see Sabrina as more than just another client? His hands linger on her skin, his breath catches when she's near.

He knows better. Soon, she'll be gone, living her life. A life that doesn't include him.

* * * *

Tempting Brooke: A Big Sky Novella

Brooke's Blooms has taken Cunningham Falls by surprise. The beautiful, innovative flower shop is trendy, with not only gorgeous flower arrangements, but also fun gifts for any occasion. This store is Brooke Henderson's deepest joy, and it means everything to her, which shows in how completely she and her little shop have been embraced by the small community of Cunningham Falls.

So, when her landlord dies and Brody Chabot saunters through her door, announcing that the building has been sold, and will soon be demolished, Brooke knows that she's in for the fight of her life. But she hasn't gotten this far by sitting back and quietly doing what she's told. *Hustle* is Brooke's middle name, and she has no intention of losing this fight, no matter how tempting Brody's smile -- and body -- is.

* * * *

No Reservations: A Fusion Novella

Chase MacKenzie is *not* the man for Maura Jenkins. A self-proclaimed life-long bachelor, and unapologetic about his distaste for monogamy, a woman would have to be a masochist to want to fall into Chase's bed.

And Maura is no masochist.

Chase has one strict rule: no strings attached. Which is fine with Maura because she doesn't even really *like* Chase. He's arrogant, cocky, and let's not forget bossy. But when he aims that crooked grin at her, she goes weak in the knees. Not that she has any intentions of falling for his charms.

Definitely not.

Well, maybe just once…

* * * *

Easy For Keeps: A Boudreaux Novella

Adam Spencer loves women. All women. Every shape and size, regardless of hair or eye color, religion or race, he simply enjoys them all. Meeting more than his fair share as the manager and head bartender of The Odyssey, a hot spot in the heart of New Orleans' French Quarter, Adam's comfortable with his lifestyle, and sees no reason to change it. A wife and kids, plus the white picket fence are not in the cards for this confirmed bachelor. Until a beautiful woman, and her sweet princess, literally knock him on his ass.

Sarah Cox has just moved to New Orleans, having accepted a position as a social worker specializing in at-risk women and children. It's a demanding, sometimes dangerous job, but Sarah is no shy wallflower. She can handle just about anything that comes at her, even the attentions of one sexy Adam Spencer. Just because he's charmed her daughter, making her think of magical kingdoms with happily ever after, doesn't mean that Sarah believes in fairy tales. But the more time she spends with the enchanting man, the more he begins to sway her into believing in forever.

Even so, when Sarah's job becomes more dangerous than any of them bargained for, will she be ripped from Adam's life forever?

* * * *

Easy With You: A With You In Seattle Novella

Nothing has ever come easy for Lila Bailey. She's fought for every good thing in her life during every day of her thirty-one years. Aside from that one night with an impossible to deny stranger a year ago, Lila is the epitome of responsible.

Steadfast. Strong.

She's pulled herself out of the train wreck of her childhood, proud to be a professor at Tulane University and laying down roots in a city she's grown to love. But when some of her female students are viciously murdered, Lila's shaken to the core and unsure of whom she can trust in New Orleans. When the police detective assigned to the murder case comes to investigate, she's even more surprised to find herself staring into the eyes of the man that made her toes curl last year.

In an attempt to move on from the tragic loss of his wife, Asher Smith moved his daughter and himself to a new city, ready for a fresh start. A damn fine police lieutenant, but new to the New Orleans force, Asher has a lot to prove to his colleagues and himself.

With a murderer terrorizing the Tulane University campus, Asher finds himself toe-to-toe with the one woman that haunts his dreams. His hands, his lips, his body know her as intimately as he's ever known anyone. As he learns her mind and heart as well, Asher wants nothing more than to keep her safe, in his bed, and in his and his daughter's lives for the long haul.

But when Lila becomes the target, can Asher save her in time, or will he lose another woman he loves?

Dream With Me
With Me In Seattle Book 13
By Kristen Proby
Coming January 21, 2020

From *New York Times* Bestselling Author Kristen Proby comes *Dream With Me*, an all-new addition to the series that has sold more than a million copies to date, her beloved With Me In Seattle Series!

Kane O'Callaghan knows what it is to have his work shown all over the world. His pieces are on display in palaces and museums, including the O'Callaghan Museum of Glass just outside of his beloved hometown of Seattle. Kane is a bit of a recluse, spending time on his farm alone and committed to his art. His life is full.

Until the day he meets her.

Wandering through museums is Anastasia Montgomery's favorite way to spend her time. Not only does art feed her soul, but it inspires her own art of designing wedding cakes. When her muse seems to be gone, she finds her again among the beauty in the museums of Seattle, and the O'Callaghan Museum of Glass is her favorite. She's never met the artist, but he must be absolutely brilliant, if he can make such beautiful things out of glass.

Bumping into a grumpy stranger at the museum wasn't in Anastasia's plan. And then discovering it was Kane himself was absolutely humiliating.

But when she sees him again at a charity fundraiser, and ends up spending an incredible, unforgettable night with the mysterious glass smith, Anastasia finds herself thinking of Kane and little else, even her precious work. Will this relationship bloom into the romance of a lifetime, or will their dreams of success get in the way of true love?

* * * *

Chapter One
~Anastasia~

"This isn't going to work."

I blow out a breath and stare at the shit-tastic mess I've scribbled on my sketch pad in disgust.

The idiots who hired me, and no, I don't always refer to my clients as idiots, didn't give me a place to start. When a couple wants a wedding cake, they usually come to me with photos they've pinned on Pinterest or found in magazines. They have colors and flowers they prefer.

They have a bloody vision.

But the people who marched into my bakery a month ago? They had none of that.

"We want you to go with your own vision," they said with wide-eyed smiles and imaginary cartoon hearts bursting over their heads. *"You're an artist, and we wouldn't dream of intruding on your process."*

I appreciate their vote of confidence. I really do. And sometimes clients are *too* stringent in what they want.

"I want exactly *this,"* some brides will say, and I have to gently remind them that I don't copy others' work.

But at least tell me what the colors of your flowers are. Throw me a damn bone!

It's not *my* wedding.

I've been in the wedding cake biz for a dozen years, and while living in California, I was lucky enough to be on Best Bites TV, designing and executing massive works of sugar that would make the most discerning of art critics weep with joy.

But now I live near my hometown of Seattle, Washington, where my family is, and I've opened a new business here. I love it. It fuels me and exhausts me, just as a person's passion should.

But today, there's nothing in my well of ideas. My muse has decided to go on vacation and didn't give me any warning.

Fucking muse.

When this happens, which isn't often, I find it's best to step away from my kitchen.

So I pack up my sketch book and pencils, get in the car, and get ready to battle Seattle traffic.

Once in the car, I call my sister, Amelia. She likes to go to museums with me, and sometimes the conversation alone will get my mind churning with new ideas.

"Hello, favorite sister," she says when she answers.

"I'm headed over to the glass museum," I say immediately. "Wanna go?"

"I would *love* to, but I'm recording today, and I have to do three videos to catch up. I'm sorry."

Lia is a super successful YouTube sensation. She films makeup tutorials and reviews products. With more than three million followers and her own makeup brand in the works, I just couldn't be prouder of her.

Not to mention, she has a new husband that keeps her more than busy.

"I get it. I miss you, though. I haven't seen you in weeks. So let's try to do a girl's night out, okay?"

"Yes, please. I'm down for that."

"Soon. Like, tomorrow night."

"Hold please." She pulls the phone away from her mouth but doesn't bother to cover it, so I can hear everything. "Wyatt? Babe, Stasia's on the phone and wants to do girl's night tomorrow night. Do we have plans? Oh, right."

I tap my fingers on the steering wheel, surprised that traffic through downtown is as light as it is.

"Hey, sorry, I can't tomorrow night. We're supposed to go to a gala for the new cardiothoracic wing at the hospital. Jace asked us weeks ago."

Just to warn you right now, our family is big and a little confusing. You might need a diagram and a PhD in astrophysics to figure out who belongs to whom and how we all fit together.

Wyatt is Amelia's husband. His brother, Jace, is the chief of staff in cardiothoracic surgery at Seattle General. Jace is a big deal. Actually, there's a lot of that in our family.

"We'll find a night to get together," I reply.

"Actually, you should come with us," Lia says, excitement in her voice. "I have dresses you can borrow, and I'll totally do your hair and makeup. It'll be fun. Say yes. Say it right now."

"Like my ass will fit in any of your dresses. Besides, I have *so much* work, Lia. I can't waste a whole day on a gala where I won't know anyone."

"You'll know me and Wyatt. And Jace and Joy. Levi and Starla will be there, too."

I sigh because deep down, I want to go. I don't get to dress up often, and I love hanging out with Wyatt's brothers and their wives. Not to mention, I never get to see my own sister.

But I have a wedding cake due on Saturday morning that's only half-decorated, and I really have to get this other cake designed so I can get to work on it first thing on Sunday.

"You're too quiet. You're thinking of a way you can ditch work so you can go, so just *do it*."

I bite my lip. If I stay up all night tonight finishing Saturday's cake, I can make it work.

"Okay. I'll go."

"Yay," Lia says with a little squeak, making me laugh. "Be at my house by noon so we can start getting ready."

"What time is the gala?"

"Eight," she says.

"It will not take eight hours to get ready."

"You're going to look like a goddess when I'm through with you," Lia promises. "See you tomorrow!"

She hangs up and I wrinkle my nose. The guilt of taking time I don't have away from work settles between my shoulder blades.

But one of the things I've been working on this year is taking more time for *me*. I moved out of California because it was killing me. I was working fifteen-hour days, seven days a week, and the result of that was illness and despair. I've battled asthma all my life, and the long hours, and some of the spices in the bakery, were hell on me. Now I have my own shop, where I can control the environment, along with how many hours a day I work, and I admit, my asthma has been better. Taking care of myself is important.

And taking one day to be with my family is part of that self-care.

Working through the night is totally worth it.

* * * *

This was the right call. Being out of the bakery today and immersed in art is exactly what I needed for a fresh perspective. Soaking in someone else's art always renews my passion for my own creativity.

It seems my muse likes to hang out in museums.

And the O'Callaghan Museum of Glass in Seattle is my very favorite of all of them.

I'm sitting on a bench in the middle of one of the exhibit rooms, soaking it all in.

I've never met Kane O'Callaghan, the artist that creates such beauty. He seems to love color, as it's splashed around me. In this room, the glass is shaped like water, waves crashing on beaches with marine life floating around it. Blues, greens and white with splashes of yellow and red here and there are all tickling my senses.

I can practically hear the water around me.

With the hair standing on my skin, I reach for my sketch pad and pencils, and with my legs crossed, I get to work.

People walk past me, but I hardly notice them. I'm consumed by the design that's taking shape in my head and on the paper. I take breaks, looking up at the glass, the color, the fluidity of the work, and then keep sketching.

I don't know if I've ever drawn a full concept so quickly.

Once I've finished, I take a deep breath and notice my chest is just beginning to feel heavy, and I glance around, surprised to see a man sitting on the bench opposite of mine, watching me with lazy brown eyes.

"Can I help you?" I ask the handsome stranger. He has dark hair, with matching stubble on his chin and eyelashes framing those almost black eyes.

"I was just going to ask you the same question," he says with a voice laced with milk chocolate.

"I'm just enjoying the exhibit," I say with a polite smile.

"Looks like you're enjoying your little drawing there," he replies, nodding at the pad in my lap. I close it and drop the smile.

"Just working," I say.

"In a museum?"

I blow out a breath of impatience. "Do you work here?"

He tilts his head to the side, watching me. "Not really."

"Then it's none of your business, is it?"

"Are you one of those people who sits in museums and copies the art there because you can't come up with original work of your own?"

"Are you always an asshole, or just today?" I retort, getting more pissed by the second. "Surely I'm not the only person in the world who gets inspired by art. In fact, I think that's the point of it."

He doesn't say anything, just blinks and watches me quietly. He's not creepy. I don't get a dangerous vibe from him. If I did, I'd run out of here alerting security.

"Can I see the sketch?" he asks, surprising me.

"It's just a—"

"I'd still like to see it." His lips tip up in a half smile that would melt far stronger women than me, and he holds his hand out, waiting for me to pass over my pad.

Finally, I flip through the pages to what I was just working on and hand it to the handsome stranger.

His eyes narrow as he examines the crude drawing. I instantly wish I'd used more color and been more thorough, but it's only supposed to be for *my* eyes. A guideline for when I start decorating the cake in just a couple of days.

"There is no water here," he says in surprise and looks up at me. "It doesn't look anything like the glass in this room."

"Why would it?" I frown. "I'm *inspired*, not copying. Besides, that's just a sketch, so when I make the final piece, I'll know what I was thinking when I thought it up."

"I see." He passes it back to me. "I like it very much. You've got a good eye."

Is that a slight accent I hear in his voice? I take a deep breath, relieved that the heaviness is gone from my lungs, and if I'm not mistaken, I can *smell* him. It's a lovely, woodsy scent that's light and masculine and, well, sexy.

"What are you doing here?" I ask.

He shrugs a shoulder and glances around the room. "Remembering, I suppose."

Before I can ask him what he means by that, a woman comes rushing into the room, her heels clicking on the hardwood floor.

"Kane, we need you in the storeroom. Now, when you see what happened, don't kill anyone."

"If a piece is broken, I can't guarantee that I won't commit murder." He glances back at me. "I guess our pleasant visit is over then."

"Wait. Are you Kane O'Callaghan?"

"One and the same." He stands and holds his hand out to shake mine. "And you are?"

"Embarrassed," I mutter as I slide my hand into his. "I won't tell you I love your work. I guess that's clear enough."

"But an artist never tires of hearing it," he replies with a wink before nodding at the frazzled woman. "Have a good time. And take all the time you need."

With that, he hurries away, and I'm left in this amazing room, flustered.

I just met Kane O'Callaghan. I showed him my sketch. He was a bit gruff, borderline rude, and I managed to call him an asshole.

"Good one, Anastasia."

About Kristen Proby

New York Times and *USA Today* bestselling author Kristen Proby has published more than thirty romance novels. She is best known for her self-published With Me In Seattle and Boudreaux series, and also works with William Morrow on the Fusion Series. Kristen lives in Montana with her husband and two cats.

Discover 1001 Dark Nights

Go to www.1001DarkNights.com to subscribe

COLLECTION ONE
FOREVER WICKED by Shayla Black
CRIMSON TWILIGHT by Heather Graham
CAPTURED IN SURRENDER by Liliana Hart
SILENT BITE: A SCANGUARDS WEDDING by Tina Folsom
DUNGEON GAMES by Lexi Blake
AZAGOTH by Larissa Ione
NEED YOU NOW by Lisa Renee Jones
SHOW ME, BABY by Cherise Sinclair
ROPED IN by Lorelei James
TEMPTED BY MIDNIGHT by Lara Adrian
THE FLAME by Christopher Rice
CARESS OF DARKNESS by Julie Kenner

COLLECTION TWO
WICKED WOLF by Carrie Ann Ryan
WHEN IRISH EYES ARE HAUNTING by Heather Graham
EASY WITH YOU by Kristen Proby
MASTER OF FREEDOM by Cherise Sinclair
CARESS OF PLEASURE by Julie Kenner
ADORED by Lexi Blake
HADES by Larissa Ione
RAVAGED by Elisabeth Naughton
DREAM OF YOU by Jennifer L. Armentrout
STRIPPED DOWN by Lorelei James
RAGE/KILLIAN by Alexandra Ivy/Laura Wright
DRAGON KING by Donna Grant
PURE WICKED by Shayla Black
HARD AS STEEL by Laura Kaye
STROKE OF MIDNIGHT by Lara Adrian
ALL HALLOWS EVE by Heather Graham
KISS THE FLAME by Christopher Rice
DARING HER LOVE by Melissa Foster
TEASED by Rebecca Zanetti
THE PROMISE OF SURRENDER by Liliana Hart

COLLECTION THREE
HIDDEN INK by Carrie Ann Ryan
BLOOD ON THE BAYOU by Heather Graham
SEARCHING FOR MINE by Jennifer Probst
DANCE OF DESIRE by Christopher Rice
ROUGH RHYTHM by Tessa Bailey
DEVOTED by Lexi Blake
Z by Larissa Ione
FALLING UNDER YOU by Laurelin Paige
EASY FOR KEEPS by Kristen Proby
UNCHAINED by Elisabeth Naughton
HARD TO SERVE by Laura Kaye
DRAGON FEVER by Donna Grant
KAYDEN/SIMON by Alexandra Ivy/Laura Wright
STRUNG UP by Lorelei James
MIDNIGHT UNTAMED by Lara Adrian
TRICKED by Rebecca Zanetti
DIRTY WICKED by Shayla Black
THE ONLY ONE by Lauren Blakely
SWEET SURRENDER by Liliana Hart

COLLECTION FOUR
ROCK CHICK REAWAKENING by Kristen Ashley
ADORING INK by Carrie Ann Ryan
SWEET RIVALRY by K. Bromberg
SHADE'S LADY by Joanna Wylde
RAZR by Larissa Ione
ARRANGED by Lexi Blake
TANGLED by Rebecca Zanetti
HOLD ME by J. Kenner
SOMEHOW, SOME WAY by Jennifer Probst
TOO CLOSE TO CALL by Tessa Bailey
HUNTED by Elisabeth Naughton
EYES ON YOU by Laura Kaye
BLADE by Alexandra Ivy/Laura Wright
DRAGON BURN by Donna Grant
TRIPPED OUT by Lorelei James

STUD FINDER by Lauren Blakely
MIDNIGHT UNLEASHED by Lara Adrian
HALLOW BE THE HAUNT by Heather Graham
DIRTY FILTHY FIX by Laurelin Paige
THE BED MATE by Kendall Ryan
NIGHT GAMES by CD Reiss
NO RESERVATIONS by Kristen Proby
DAWN OF SURRENDER by Liliana Hart

COLLECTION FIVE
BLAZE ERUPTING by Rebecca Zanetti
ROUGH RIDE by Kristen Ashley
HAWKYN by Larissa Ione
RIDE DIRTY by Laura Kaye
ROME'S CHANCE by Joanna Wylde
THE MARRIAGE ARRANGEMENT by Jennifer Probst
SURRENDER by Elisabeth Naughton
INKED NIGHTS by Carrie Ann Ryan
ENVY by Rachel Van Dyken
PROTECTED by Lexi Blake
THE PRINCE by Jennifer L. Armentrout
PLEASE ME by J. Kenner
WOUND TIGHT by Lorelei James
STRONG by Kylie Scott
DRAGON NIGHT by Donna Grant
TEMPTING BROOKE by Kristen Proby
HAUNTED BE THE HOLIDAYS by Heather Graham
CONTROL by K. Bromberg
HUNKY HEARTBREAKER by Kendall Ryan
THE DARKEST CAPTIVE by Gena Showalter

Also from 1001 Dark Nights:

TAME ME by J. Kenner
THE SURRENDER GATE By Christopher Rice
SERVICING THE TARGET By Cherise Sinclair
TEMPT ME by J. Kenner

On Behalf of 1001 Dark Nights,

Liz Berry and M.J. Rose would like to thank ~

Steve Berry
Doug Scofield
Kim Guidroz
Jillian Stein
InkSlinger PR
Dan Slater
Asha Hossain
Chris Graham
Chelle Olson
Kasi Alexander
Jessica Johns
Dylan Stockton
Richard Blake
and Simon Lipskar

Made in the USA
San Bernardino, CA
08 December 2019